He was taking off the soiled shirt and a broad, tanned chest and rippling shoulders were being revealed. Davina had a sudden aching longing to be held up against him, to be close to the strength and sensual grace of him.

Observing her with the bright hazel gaze that missed nothing, he said, 'The feeling is mutual. You are very beautiful dressed, Davina, but I would imagine that naked you are divine.'

At that moment it was as if there was only the two of them in the world. Everything else that had gone before was forgotten. There was only desire—sweet, demanding desire. A different hunger was in them now. Food was forgotten and, taking his hand, she led him towards the lofty curving staircase.

Abigail Gordon loves to write about the fascinating combination of medicine and romance from her home in a Cheshire village. She is active in local affairs and is even called upon to write the script for the annual village pantomime! Her eldest son is a hospital manager and helps with all her medical research. As part of a close-knit family, she treasures having two of her sons living close by and the third one not too far away. This gives her the added pleasure of being able to watch her delightful grandchildren growing up.

Recent titles by the same author:

THE GP'S SECRET

BY
ABIGAIL GORDON

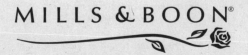

*First published in Great Britain 2004
Harlequin Mills & Boon Limited,
Eton House, 18-24 Paradise Road, Richmond, Surrey TW9 1SR*

© Abigail Gordon 2004

ISBN 0 263 83876 5

*Set in Times Roman 10½ on 12 pt.
03-0104-50990*

*Printed and bound in Spain
by Litografía Rosés, S.A., Barcelona*

CHAPTER ONE

IT WAS crisp and clear. A typical April morning in the valley, with the peaks standing out darkly against a pale blue sky. As Davina reined Jasper to a halt she could see a furniture van down below outside the surgery and her heart began to beat faster. The scene had a message of its own. It meant change. Change for the locals, but even more so for herself.

The new doctor was in the process of moving into the practice and as a trainee GP employed there she was going to be affected by what was happening. Usually calm and collected, she was finding the sight down below unnerving.

Her thoughts were winging back over the years to the day when she'd told Andrew Swinburn, who'd been the family GP for as long as she could remember, that she was going to medical school to become a doctor.

He'd beamed his approval and had said, 'I hope that you'll come back to us once you're qualified, Davina. I'm not getting any younger, you know, and to have a daughter of the valley, and you in particular, working beside me would be very acceptable. That is, if you're not intending going into a hospital situation.'

She'd shaken long blonde tresses and told him, 'I'll be back, Dr Swinburn. I want to be a GP and the valley is as good a place as any to start. Aunt Grace and my dad are like you, they aren't getting any younger either. They've always been there for me and someday I will need to be there for them. As you know, Dad has become

5

very arthritic of late. Running the stables is getting too much for him.'

When he'd nodded and said, 'Aye, that father of yours has always been unbending in one way or another,' she'd known he'd been referring to what had happened to her mother all those years ago.

He'd thrown her out when Davina had been only small because she'd fallen in love with another man and no one had seen her since. Her father's widowed sister, Grace, had moved in and provided the loving care that had cushioned her niece from being a bewildered and frightened five-year-old to coltish adolescence and from there to independent womanhood.

Michael Richards was a taciturn man of few words when he brought his wife from the softer greenery of her native Sussex to live in the rugged moorland of Cheshire, and after her departure he had even less to say.

He never married again. Never even considered it. Not with his pleasant, energetic sister to provide the home comforts for himself and his motherless daughter. The fact that Grace might sometimes want a life of her own never entered his head and because she loved Davina she rarely complained.

Michael Richards's marriage was a mistake from the start. His wife, Isabel, was a gentle dreamer, lost and miserable amongst the towering Pennines, and when she and Davina went on a short visit to her parents down south Isabel fell in love with her childhood sweetheart all over again and it went on from there, with the new man in her life visiting the area surreptitiously when it was safe for them to meet.

Her father caught them one night when he returned from a horse sale, and that had been the last Davina saw of her mother. It had always hurt that Isabel had made no effort to see her over the years, in spite of Michael having threatened to kill the pair of them if they ever showed their faces in the valley again. But the hurt was eased by having Grace there to love her, and as time had passed it was she that became the mother figure in her life.

Grace and Davina learnt to let her father's grim silences wash over them and when he died in Davina's last year at college the two women felt as if a great weight had been lifted from their lives.

By the time she graduated the stables had been sold, with the exception of her own mount, Jasper, and according to the instructions in her father's will the money was put in a trust until such time as she was ready to buy herself into a practice.

Davina had inherited Isabel's tall slenderness and the pale gold hair and blue eyes, but her aunt had often told her that the resemblance ended there. Davina was a product of her age, clever, confident, and career-minded, and as she sat astride Jasper, high on the hillside, it was her career that was uppermost in her mind.

Newly qualified and keen to become involved in general medical practice, she *had* come back to the valley and for the last six months Davina had been working happily alongside Andrew Swinburn.

His partner had recently moved to pastures new and so her arrival at the practice had been fortuitous as far as the elderly GP was concerned, but he'd reckoned without human frailty.

A mild heart attack some weeks ago had made him take stock and Davina had been devastated to learn that Andrew had decided to retire and was being replaced by a GP from a practice in a market town some miles away.

'The Primary Care Trust have agreed to the new set-up,' Andrew had told her, 'and I've given the fellow an excellent report on you, so once everything has settled down I think you'll agree that I've done the right thing. It's no use waiting until I'm past it before hanging up my stethoscope, Davina. It's just unfortunate that we're having to part company so soon.'

She'd agreed wholeheartedly with that. It had been great to be practising medicine amongst her own folk under the guidance of a man she'd known all her life, and even if some parts of the practice were due for modernisation it didn't prevent Andrew Swinburn and his staff from giving good service to the villagers.

But now a new broom was about to appear and new brooms were known to sweep clean. She would dearly like to know what lay ahead. If what was going on in the deserted main street of the village was anything to go by, her questions were soon going to be answered.

So far her aunt knew nothing of the changes that were about to take place at the village practice. With the chains that had bound her to her brother now broken, she'd gone on a world cruise with an old school friend and when they'd chatted briefly at the various ports of call Davina had said nothing about Andrew Swinburn's retirement. If she knew, Grace would be concerned on her behalf and Davina didn't want matters back home to intrude into her much-deserved holiday.

Since Michael Richards's death the two women had continued to live harmoniously in Heatherlea, the old stone house that had been Davina's home for as long as she could remember.

It stood high on the hillside, challenging the elements with the same uncompromising facade her father had always shown, but she'd often thought wistfully that Heatherlea always took her into its embrace when she came home, which was more than could have been said of her father.

From her vantage point on the hill she could see the men who'd come with the van carrying furniture and packing cases in at the side door of the surgery, and instead of going home for breakfast after her early morning ride on Jasper, Davina decided that there was no point in delaying. The moment had arrived to introduce herself to the new doctor and what better time than at this early hour when half the village was still asleep?

Rowan Westlake was tired, grimy and on edge. The tiredness and grime were due to having had a Saturday morning surgery the previous day, followed by packing up his possessions, which had taken him until the early hours of the morning, and then in the spring dawn setting off behind the furniture van to his new life.

His being on edge was for a different reason. When he'd viewed the practice some weeks ago he hadn't taken all that much notice of the living accommodation above it. His mind had been on the size of the working area and the facilities, but today the old flowered carpet and green-washed walls had registered and with the memory, as clear as crystal, of the elegant apartment he'd left behind, he was beginning to wonder why he'd moved into this mausoleum.

Yet even as he asked himself the question he knew the answer. He'd moved to this place for two reasons. Firstly because he was tired of the impersonality of a large practice. He was too much of an individualist for that sort of thing. And secondly he'd come here to try to right a wrong. But that part of his plans was going to have to wait until he'd settled into the village. It had been going on for a long time. A few more weeks wouldn't make any difference.

He was beside the van, supervising the unloading of his two favourite pictures, when he heard the clip-clop of horse's hoofs on the cobbled forecourt of the surgery. When he looked up he saw that he was being observed by a blue-eyed blonde mounted on a sprightly chestnut.

She was wearing jodhpurs, a smart pale blue sweater, which clung to the firm globes of her breasts like a second skin, and the usual protective headgear, and as he met her cool appraisal his edginess increased.

He was dressed in an old shirt, baggy corduroy trousers, and looked as grimy as he felt. If this was one of the county set passing by she could do just that he thought...pass by.

'Yes?' he enquired with clipped brevity.

She swung a leg over the horse's back and, raising a pair of neat buttocks off the saddle, dismounted. Then, with hand outstretched, she announced, 'I'm Davina Richards, trainee GP at the practice.'

He felt as if the ground was rocking beneath his feet as he offered his own sweaty paw. This was incredible. He'd thought she mightn't be hard to find if she was still living in the area, but had never dreamt it would be this easy. He hadn't needed to look for her. *She had come to him!* Before he'd even moved in, here she was, smiling across at him as she waited for him to acknowledge her greeting.

He was gathering his wits.

'Rowan Westlake,' he said, finding his voice. 'Andrew Swinburn's successor. He told me all about you, but I hadn't been given a name.'

Thinking of the ghastly decor in the rooms above, he wondered if he would have moved here if he *had* been given a name. His quest would have been over before it had begun and he could have chosen a less rural practice. But there'd been something about the windswept grandeur of the area that had appealed to him, and here he was, for better or worse. He'd bought the place, lock, stock and barrel, and for the time being would have to put up with the antimacassars and aspidistras.

'I saw that you were moving in and thought I ought to come down and introduce myself,' she was saying. She turned and waved vaguely in the direction of the hillside behind the practice. 'I live up there,' she said, and then, in a more positive tone, added, 'Is there anything I can do to help? Have you eaten? I haven't had breakfast yet. You're welcome to join me.'

His irritation wasn't decreasing. She was cool and classy and she looked more like a tramp than a GP.

'Thanks for the offer,' he told her. 'The removers and I had something to eat at a motorway service station on our way here and I don't really want to break off until we've finished, then I'll get a bite at the pub.'

'Sure,' she said easily, and wondered if he felt that she was crowding him on such short acquaintance. 'In that case I'll be off, then.'

'There is one thing you could do for me, if you don't mind,' he said as she turned away.

'What is it?'

'Could you spare me an hour this evening? I should be straight by then and perhaps we could have a chat about the practice. Such as the staff and the procedures that are in place. It would make me feel better organised tomorrow morning when the new week begins and we are besieged by Monday's patients.'

'Yes, of course,' she agreed. 'I've nothing planned for tonight. What time do you want me here?'

'Whenever it's convenient. I'm aware that I'm breaking into your weekend.'

She was about to remount. 'No problem. I'll be down as soon as I've eaten.'

He nodded.

'Fine.'

As she rode off, with back straight as a ramrod and head held high, he watched her until she'd disappeared from sight. He'd been able to see a resemblance, but the hat had obscured most of her hair, and part of the time her face had been in shadow, but if he'd had any doubts the name would have clinched it.

Rowan felt that *he* hadn't shown up in a very good light. His appearance had been far from appetising, his manner abrupt, and he'd refused her polite invitation. Hopefully, tonight he would redeem himself.

As Jasper picked his way back up the hillside, Davina was reliving those moments in the street below. Rowan Westlake was going to make his presence felt. She could feel it in her bones. She sensed that she hadn't caught him at his best, but time would tell how good a doctor he was.

Andrew Swinburn had known all his patients by name, wined with them, dined with them and hadn't felt the need to dress up for them. An open-necked shirt, well-washed cardigan and infrequent visits to the village barber had been his style, and today his successor hadn't looked much better, but he was the kind of man who would look good in anything.

The dark hazel eyes, which for some reason had avoided hers, the hair as black as ebony and the firm jawline had been just as spectacular as the trim, lean frame of him.

Their more impressionable women patients would be queuing up for the pleasure of having Rowan Westlake's finger on their pulse. As for herself, she was anticipating that the increased demands of the job would be enough to keep her mind off the new doctor's attractions.

Her love life came and went. She'd had a few dates while at college. Been out a couple of times with Jack Morrison, a husky farmer's son from up the valley, and was at present keeping at bay the amorous intentions of Clive Holden, the long-haired amateur sculptor who owned the craft shop in the village.

None of the friendships had been serious. Her heart was still intact. She was in love with the job and so far hadn't met up with any competition. What about Rowan Westlake? she wondered. There was always a woman in the life of a man as well put together as he.

There'd been no sign of a family milling around him, or even a wife, but there was nothing to say they weren't on their way. Andrew had told her that he was moving from a bigger practice than theirs in one of the big towns.

'Struck me as the sort of fellow who would want to sail his own ship,' he'd said. 'Plenty of authority and get up and go about him.'

Davina had groaned and the elderly GP had enquired, 'What's the problem?'

'The last thing I fancy is working with a whip-cracker.'

He'd smiled. 'You'll cope. I've seen you at work and you've the makings of a good doctor, Davina. Don't let anybody ever tell you otherwise.'

And now it was testing time, she told herself as she let herself into the empty house.

The main street of the village was a livelier place at seven o'clock in the evening than it had been that morning. A group of hikers, down from the tops now that the light was fading, were trooping into the pub, Bridget Brierley, the crotchety widow who lived in the cottage next to it, was about to take her dog for its evening exercise and a couple of teenagers were scuffling about with a ball.

As she approached the craft shop Clive Holden was putting up the shutters and he called across, 'Hi, Davina. I see the new doc's arrived. Have you met him yet?'

'Yes,' she told him, slowing her steps.

'What's he like?'

'Seems all right. I think he might be just what this place needs.'

Whether Rowan Westlake would be what *she* needed was another matter. She might have been feeling less tense if he'd been a bit more nondescript, but for some reason the village was about to be served by a go-ahead townie type, if what Andrew Swinburn had said was correct.

'Really?' Clive commented. 'New blood and all that, then?' And as he liked to know what was going on locally, he went on, 'I might call in and introduce myself some time tomorrow.'

Davina eyed him dubiously. Clive was a gossip who liked the sound of his own voice. She didn't want him doing a breakdown of her lifestyle for the new doctor, along with everyone else's in the village.

'By all means,' she told him, 'but do remember, Clive, Rowan Westlake has a few very busy days ahead of him. I don't think he'll have much time for cosy chats.'

'He'll see me,' he said confidently. 'I have one or two minor ailments I can present for his attention.'

Such as an inflated ego or a loose tongue, she thought as she went on her way. He'd once had the nerve to say to her, 'I believe that your mother disappeared years ago and that in those times some folk thought your father had done away with her.'

She'd stared at him in horrified amazement. It was the first she'd heard of it and Grace had found her sobbing her heart out.

'Rubbish!' she'd said angrily. 'There is always gossip. Especially in a community such as this. We'd have had the police round if there had been any suspicion of that. Richard was a strange man, but if he'd done anything as wicked as that he would have done it openly. Clive Holden will get the length of my tongue the next time I see him.'

'But he's got the story from somewhere,' she'd protested tearfully.

'Probably heard it from that wicked old father of his,' her aunt had said. 'He was always sniffing around your mother from what I've been told.'

It had been one of the occasions when the past had reared its head and she had insisted that Grace let the matter drop. The fear and pain of all that time ago had been soothed away by her aunt's loving care over the years and now it lay muffled deep in Davina's subconscious.

When he opened the door to her Rowan experienced it again—the feeling of stunned amazement—but this time it came not from the surprise of finding her. It was the resemblance that had him rocking. The physical likeness was much more evident tonight.

The riding clothes had been replaced by a pair of jeans that fitted her snugly and a low-cut sweater. With the absence of the hat her features were clearer. The eyes were the same colour, the hair the same pale gold and the mouth, although firmer, similarly sweetly curving.

As she smiled across at him, waiting to be invited inside, he had to swallow hard to hold back tears. It had been a strange and unnerving day so far and was continuing to be so. But he couldn't keep Davina Richards standing on the doorstep for ever and, stepping back, he managed a smile.

'Do come in, Davina,' he said. 'And thanks again for coming.'

He had his doctor's hat on after that. Time was short. They had a lot to discuss. Such as the patients' records system, facilities, procedures under the NHS…and budgets. The irksome things that doctors dreaded.

Davina explained about Ann and Rosemary, the two part-time receptionists, both of them middle-aged. Lucy Graham, the practice nurse, single mother of a teenage boy. Megan, the district nurse, who'd worked in the valley's health care programme almost as long as Andrew Swinburn had, and the elderly cleaner, Betty Goodwin.

He listened to everything she said and then with his keen hazel gaze no longer avoiding hers said, 'There'll be changes, Davina. You do understand that? It's been a relief to find that the surgery is a lot more modern than that antediluvian flat upstairs, but there will still be alterations I need to make staffwise and in procedures to increase efficiency.'

She eyed him steadily.

'Obviously, but do, please, give those who work here time to adjust before you make any changes amongst them. Jobs are hard to come by in places like this and having to travel to the town for employment is expensive.'

She took a deep breath.

'What about me?'

'What *about* you?'

'Am *I* going to fit in?'

'I would expect so. Dr Swinburn informed me that you're keen and capable…and you know the place and the folk here. I'm expecting you to be invaluable, and I'm sure you'll learn a lot as well.'

She pulled a wry face.

'Please, don't say that. It will make me nervous.'

'Nonsense,' he said briskly as he turned out the surgery lights. 'We're going to take the valley by storm, you and I. They will have never seen such health care. And now I'm going to walk you home. I'd have driven you there but the car is still full of stuff from the move, so we'll venture into the moonlit night and you can show me where you live.'

Davina looked at Rowan in surprise.

'There's no need for that. You've had an exhausting day…and I know the way blindfold.'

'Maybe you do, but if you think I'm going to let you go home alone at this time of night, after having brought you down here, you're very much mistaken.'

It was true, what he'd said. He wasn't going to let her go home in the darkened countryside on her own. She might have done it before, but it wasn't going to happen while he was around. And there was another reason why he wanted to go with her. He wanted to see where she lived. He'd heard about Heatherlea often enough and now the opportunity was there for him to see the place for himself, even if it wasn't the best time of day to be seeing it.

As they walked together up the hillside Davina was uncomfortable. It hadn't been many hours since she'd sat astride Jasper and watched them unloading his furniture,

and since then they'd spent three hours alone in the surgery and now he was walking her home. It was all moving a bit too fast even though it was nice to be fussed
over by the opposite sex for once.

When they came upon the house, standing out starkly
in the moonlight, Rowan stopped and she eyed him ques-
tioningly.

'What is it?'

He didn't reply, struck dumb by the strangeness of the
moment. The girl beside him had lived in this house all
her life, he was thinking, and he hadn't even known she
existed.

'I'm just taking in the atmosphere,' he told her, not
without truth. 'The Pennines hold a fascination for me.
You can probably tell by my accent that I don't come
from these parts. I'm a Southerner, but I studied medicine
in Sheffield and have stayed amongst the peaks ever
since.'

'And where are your family?' she asked.

'I haven't any,' he said, and there was something in
his voice that told her she wasn't going to get to know
much else about him.

Nevertheless, she asked Rowan if he would be living
alone in the flat above the practice and he seemed somewhat bemused by the question.

'Well, yes,' he replied. 'What were you envisaging?'

'I thought that perhaps you might have a family who
would be following you.'

'No way,' he said. 'I wouldn't bring a wife and children to live in a flat such as the one above the surgery.
It wouldn't be big enough for one thing and women who
marry doctors are often known to have cause for regret.
Long hours, night calls, patients who treat them as unpaid
locums. He who travels alone gets there more quickly.'

She had to smile at his jaundiced view.

'What about *men* who marry doctors?'

'They get a better deal,' he told her with an answering smile. 'Their own medic to see to all their aches and pains. I hope you're not in that sort of situation yourself.'

'If you mean, am *I* married? The answer is no,' she told him. 'And it's not for the reasons that you've come up with. I've never met anybody I want to spend the rest of my life with.'

'Me neither,' he said absently, as he thought that Davina must have met every eligible guy in the valley in her job. She was eye-catching, to say the least. What was wrong with them? Hadn't they got warm blood in their veins?

'The house is in darkness,' he remarked, with a not unexpected change of subject. 'Surely you don't live alone?'

Davina smiled in the gloom.

'No. I live with my Aunt Grace. She's on a cruise at the moment. My father died last year and my mother... er...she was, er...'

Deprived of her child, he thought grimly, made to pay in the most painful way imaginable.

'No need to tell me your life history,' he said quickly. 'I was just concerned to think of you living alone in such a big place.'

What was he on about? Rowan was asking himself. He was here to right a wrong, not to start theorising about Davina's living conditions. And in any case, he wanted to know her better before he said anything. Words once spoken could never be taken back, and they had a practice to run.

'I'll be fine now,' she said, interrupting his thoughts, 'and thanks for walking me home, Dr Westlake.'

His teeth flashed whitely in the moonlight as he smiled.

'That's my ''in surgery'' title. For the rest of the time my name's Rowan.'

'Right. I'll remember that…Rowan,' Davina said hesitantly. Taking a bunch of keys out of her pocket, she opened an iron gate and made her way past clumps of daffodils nodding sleepily in a well-kept garden.

He waited until she'd gone inside and then turned and made his way back to the village. There'd been one or two eventful days in his life recently, he thought as the surgery loomed up on the skyline, but today had been in a class of its own, and now all he wanted to do was sleep, so that he would be bright-eyed and bushy-tailed tomorrow.

Rowan wasn't the only one who was feeling it had been an eventful day. Alone in the house Davina was thinking back over its happenings, from the moment she'd seen the furniture van on the street below to their meeting on the practice forecourt, followed by the evening spent as a 'getting to know the routine' time for Rowan. And last, but not least, had been their walk home in the chilly, moonlit night.

When she'd gone down to introduce herself she'd anticipated those few minutes being all the time they would have together until the following day, but it hadn't turned out like that and she was happy that it hadn't. Tomorrow it would be all systems go and she was thankful that she'd had the chance to get to know him as much as she had.

Her upbeat feeling about it lasted until she saw Rowan's expression the following morning. The good night's sleep he'd been looking forward to had eluded him, tired as he'd been. He'd been kept awake by various things. Strange noises that he'd thought gloomily could be bats in the attic, cows mooing in the field across the way and the hot-water system gurgling like a drowning man. But the main thing that had made sleep hard to come by had been the memory of a cool voice saying, 'I'm Davina Richards.'

His life had changed in that moment. So had hers, though she wasn't to know it yet. And where before he'd been anxious to find a suitable time to tell her who he was, in the dark hours of the night he'd begun to think that he wanted to get to know her without the past hanging over them.

It hadn't jollied him up any when he'd gone to get the morning paper from the newsagent's on the corner and had been accosted by a guy with long hair and a beard who'd wanted advice on how to treat an ingrown toenail.

He'd suggested a visit to the chiropodist but the fellow had insisted that Dr Swinburn had always sorted him out and Rowan hadn't been able to ignore the hint of reproof in the comment.

'Then I suggest you make an appointment at the surgery,' he'd told him, and had gone to wrestle with the apartment's old gas cooker with an eye to cooking himself some breakfast.

CHAPTER TWO

'IS EVERYTHING all right?' Davina asked when she arrived at the surgery to find Rowan looking frayed around the edges expression-wise though far from frayed in every other way.

In a smart suit, shirt and tie, he was immaculate, and she thought that staff and patients when they arrived were going to be impressed by the outfit, even if they weren't too happy with the expression.

He gave a rueful smile.

'Yes. I suppose so. On top of what was a very restless night, some fellow with long hair and a beard wanted a consultation about an ingrown toenail while I was in the newsagent's, which didn't go down too well. And there were all sorts of background noises while I was trying to get some sleep. This place isn't haunted, is it?'

He could have told her that meeting her so soon and so unexpectedly hadn't exactly been the forerunner of restful sleep either and he could imagine the questions that would bring forth.

'I doubt it,' she told him laughingly, 'although the valley has its share of ghosts and legends. And the man in the newsagent's would almost certainly be Clive Holden, who owns the craft shop in the village. I saw him last night when I was on my way here and he was threatening to come in for a chat. I told him you would be too busy for that sort of thing, but I'm afraid that when it comes to being insensitive he's in the top ratings.'

'Well, he's had his ''chat'', as far as I'm concerned,'

Rowan said firmly. 'He knows the procedure if he wants to make an appointment.'

Before the surgery doors were opened to the public he asked Davina to gather the staff together for a quick word, and as he addressed them she had to hand it to him.

He was crisp and businesslike in what he had to say, warning of changes to come. But he must have remembered her comment from the previous night, when she'd asked him to give the staff time to get used to any new routines he might have in mind before he made any judgements on their performances, and so his manner was also pleasant and encouraging.

By the time the day was ready to get under way the tension his arrival had brought with it had lessened and Rosemary, the receptionist on duty, summed up Davina's own feelings when she said, 'I see Dr Westlake as a very interesting, mysterious man.'

The waiting room was packed and as Davina was making her way to the smallest of the two consulting rooms to prepare to greet her first patient, he said, 'So, is it curiosity that's got them all out of bed or a sudden plague of bad health?'

'A bit of both, I would imagine,' she replied. 'And before we get bogged down with the sick and suffering here, what about the house calls afterwards? Do you want us to split them, or do them together until you get to know people?'

'Depends how many there are. If there's only a few we'll team up. If there are a lot we'll have to split them,' he said levelly. 'I'll make a decision on that later.'

Davina felt as she had the previous day when she'd invited him to join her for breakfast, that maybe he thought she was too pushy.

The fact of the matter was that she would be pleased to introduce him to their housebound patients, the two of them doing the rounds together. But she supposed it was only fair if he thought that any suggestions of that nature should be coming from him.

Strangely, her first patient of the day was someone she didn't know. So much for her boast of being on familiar terms with everyone in the community.

The smart, elderly woman seating herself opposite was explaining, 'I've just moved into the area, Doctor. I registered with this practice only last week and here I am. No sooner one of your patients than I'm needing your services.'

Davina smiled.

'That's what we're here for, er…' She glanced down at the patient's record card that had come through from Reception. 'Mrs Boulton. What seems to be the problem?'

Elaine Boulton grimaced. 'I'm one of many women who have unidentifiable pelvic pain. It is always there. Sometimes more severe than others. I've had scans, X-rays, biopsies, anal examinations, but no cause for the problem ever shows up. I've moved up from the Newcastle area and my consultant there was about to recommend me to a pain clinic as a last resort. He's now beginning to think that the discomfort is being caused by nerve impulses, possibly connected with the spine and not easily treatable. Hence the suggestion of the pain clinic.

'I'm told that those sort of places don't just hand out painkillers. They are aware of the newest and most sophisticated remedies and on occasion have actually recommended that a nerve that is causing agony to the patient be severed.

'I'm willing to try anything. It's been going on for years and I'm at the end of my tether. I'm here today to ask if an appointment with a pain clinic in this area can be arranged for me, as there was no point in the Tyneside hospital that I was with going ahead when I was due to move down here any day.'

Davina had listened carefully to what she had said. It was the first case of its kind she had come across. There was always a cause for whatever ailed the patient, but the ease with which the source was identified could vary greatly. This woman, who was obviously no softy, was telling her that she was in continual pain and the medical profession couldn't tell her why.

'I've taken note of what you've said,' she told her, 'but before we can refer you to a pain clinic we have to have your notes. They will tell us what kind of treatment you've had in the past, which consultants you've seen. Once we have that information, we can act.'

'I'll ask our receptionist to get in touch with your previous practice and request them to let us have the information by whatever means will be the quickest, and as soon as we have it we'll be in touch.'

That brought a weary smile to the patient's face.

'Thank you,' she said. 'The pain has been at its worst over the last couple of weeks. The stress of the move hasn't helped. I noticed that someone here has been going through the same process. I saw the new doctor moving in yesterday.'

Davina wasn't going to be drawn on that one. Rowan had already had one member of the village overdoing the interest bit so to nip in the bud any further comments she said pleasantly, 'Yes, indeed,' adding quickly, 'I see from your address that you've moved into Top Meadow Farm.'

Elaine Boulton sighed.

'Yes. It's my son's place. His wife has left him and I've come to look after my grandchild.'

Davina eyed her in surprise. She knew the Boultons and would have thought the marriage was solid, but obviously it wasn't. It sounded like history repeating itself. Another mother who'd left her child behind.

'So we need to get you sorted as soon as possible, then, don't we?' she said with a sympathetic smile. 'It sounds as if you're going to be a busy lady.'

If she'd been unfamiliar with her first patient, it wasn't so with her second. Harold Wagstaffe was the leader of the local rambling club and well known amongst those who walked the surrounding countryside in all weathers. He was sixty-five years old, fit and wiry, from a family whose forebears had always lived in the valley. Usually he had a smile for her, but not today. He was limping and immediately launched into a gloomy explanation of how it had come about.

'I'm as surefooted as a mountain goat out there on the moors,' he said as he lowered himself onto the seat across the desk from Davina. 'Never even turned my ankle in all the years I've been leading the ramblers, until Saturday night.'

'And what happened on Saturday night?' she asked.

'I twisted my foot in the middle of a waltz at the church hall. Me, king of the wild frontier, went sprawling! It wouldn't have been so bad if it had been a quickstep, but a waltz! Flat on the floor in the middle of a sedate waltz.'

Davina was trying not to smile. Harold obviously thought that his reputation was at stake.

'And it's bothering you, I take it?'

'Aye. It's swollen and hurts when I put my foot to the floor. I've kept thinking over the weekend that I should have gone to Casualty. I've a walk organised for Thursday and I've never missed one yet.'

'Then you'd better take your shoe and sock off,' she suggested.

He winced when she touched the badly swollen foot and Davina decided an X-ray was needed. It was either a very bad sprain or there was a fracture somewhere amongst the many bones of the foot.

'You're going to say I have to go to the hospital, aren't you?' he said dolefully when she'd finished examining the swelling.

'Yes. I'm afraid I am. If I were you, I'd cancel the walk you've got planned this week. Whether it's a sprain or a fracture, you're going to need to keep off the foot until the inflammation goes down.'

'It was the wife's fault,' he grumbled. 'If she hadn't insisted I have a dance with her sister Mary, I wouldn't have come to grief, but that woman thinks she's Ginger Rogers in size eights and she tripped me up.'

After Harold had gone to inform his wife that she was going to have to drive him to the hospital, the younger end of the community began to arrive. As she examined a child who almost certainly was developing chickenpox, followed by a mother with a young baby that was vomiting its food back all the time, Davina wondered how Rowan was finding his first morning in a Pennine practice.

He had thrown off his earlier fatigue and was at his efficient best as he mentally separated those who'd basically come to have a look at the new doctor from those who would have been there no matter who was handing out the medicine, so in need of treatment were they.

So far he was happy with his assistant. He had decided

that he was going to have to keep Davina's presence in his life in separate compartments. He had to be objective about her, otherwise he wasn't going to be able to think clearly about what he had to do. His main aim was to prevent any more hurt and now that he'd met her, what had seemed clear-cut and obvious before wasn't any more.

On first acquaintance she appeared to be a well-adjusted, dedicated young doctor. Attractive beyond doubt, happy in her home environment, and for the present he was prepared to let it rest at that.

When he'd decided to settle in the valley he'd known it had been for two reasons. One, because he liked the place and, two, because Davina might still be living in the area, and if she wasn't, it would be a good place to start making enquiries. The last thing he'd expected had been that she would turn out to be part of his working life as well as the past.

As patients came and went he knew he liked these down-to-earth northern folk. He always had. That was why he'd never gone back down south since his student days. Here in the valley they knew their roots and cherished them. But would Davina want to pull up hers when she heard what he had to say?

There were quite a few house calls to be made and when they met for a quick coffee after surgery he said, 'We'll take half each, Davina. I think I can manage on my own.'

He watched her colour rise and knew he'd been tactless. She would be thinking that she was being put in her place when the truth of the matter was that he wanted to keep her at a distance until he was properly settled in.

For one thing, she'd said that her aunt was away and he'd like to get to know Grace before he blundered into their lives. It was possible that both of them would look askance at him when they discovered who he was, but to him a promise was a promise kept, and if that was how it turned out he would have to accept it.

But as he glanced across at Davina, drinking her coffee and swinging long legs as she perched on a high stool in the kitchen at the back of the surgery, he knew that he didn't want the message he'd brought to cut him off from her. They had the job to think of, for one thing. Disharmony between them would do the practice no good. But there was more to it than that. More than family ties. More than righting old wrongs. He wanted her to like him for himself.

She was young, apparently carefree and her golden fairness and direct blue gaze were not to be ignored. Davina was also free according to what she'd said when they'd been discussing his own state of play in the marriage stakes. Maybe her attractions were taken for granted by those who lived in the quiet rural backwater where she'd chosen to practise medicine.

That thought lasted until he'd drunk the coffee and was ready to start his rounds. Davina had preceded him and when he went outside she was chatting to a young farmer type who was looking down at her from the raised seat of a tractor. Rowan stepped back out of sight as he heard the man say, 'They tell me that old Andrew's been replaced by a city smoothie.'

'Do they?' she said coolly. 'And who might "they" be?'

'Some of those who've seen him this morning.'

'Am I to take it, then, that these people are passing judgement on Dr. Westlake because he isn't wearing an old cardigan and needing a haircut? Have they never heard of progress?'

Rowan smiled in the shadows. Whatever *she* thought about him, Davina was putting 'country boy' in his place.

'So when are we going out again?' he was asking.

'When you can promise not to get fresh,' she told him, and now Rowan found himself frowning.

So the men of the valley weren't entirely blind. There was at least one who lusted after the junior doctor. Deciding that the conversation needed to be nipped in the bud, he stepped forward.

After giving the man on the tractor a casual nod, Rowan said to her, 'I know I said we'd do the house visits separately, Davina, but I think we might do the first one on my list together. From the patient's notes it sounds as if your presence might come in handy.'

'I'm taking it that you are acquainted with the Warrenders?' he questioned, as the farmer type, having taken the hint, went trundling off down the road on his unwieldy vehicle.

It had been a spur-of-the-moment suggestion, born of the awareness that he'd been abrupt before, and he was watching to see how she would take it after what he'd said previously.

Her face brightened but her voice was sombre as she told him, 'Yes. John was a peak warden until the cancer made its presence known last summer. He's been very positive about it so far, but the chemo isn't working and he's now so weak and ill it can't be long. I *would* like to be there for support when you tell him that he's only got a short time.'

Rowan's face was grave.

'It's no respector of persons, is it? The man isn't yet forty and he's dying of lung cancer. The elderly are the ones who have the best chance as the illness doesn't progress so fast in the old.'

When an anxious-looking woman showed them into the neat front bedroom of a cottage beside the local reservoir, the man in the bed stared at them in surprise.

'Who's this that you've brought to see me, Davina?' he asked, between bouts of coughing.

'This is Dr Westlake,' she told him. 'He's taken over the practice as from yesterday, John.'

'And he's not brought any good news with him if the expression on your faces are anything to go by.'

'Hello, there, Mr Warrender,' Rowan said, stepping up to the bed. 'How are you today?'

'He's weak as a kitten, Doctor,' his wife answered for him. 'Nothing they give him does any good.'

Rowan nodded.

'No,' he agreed. 'The chemotherapy you've been having hasn't worked, I'm afraid, John. What's important now is that we make you as comfortable as possible. We were wondering if you'd like to consider a hospice. They would give you the very best care, and make life more comfortable for both you and your wife.'

The patient shook his head. His glance was on his wife who had turned away to hide her tears.

'Thanks for the suggestion, Doctor, but I'd rather die in my own bed.'

'At least let us get you into hospital for a couple of days so they can draw off some of the fluid that is accumulating,' he persisted, but again there was a shake of the head.

'It's the quality of life that counts when you're as poorly as I am, not the quantity. I've known for days that I'm on my way out. It would only give me a short respite and what's the point of that?'

'If your husband changes his mind about a hospice, let us know, Mrs Warrender,' Rowan said to the man's wife as they went downstairs. 'He's right in thinking that he hasn't got long and those sorts of places really do make the patient as comfortable as is humanly possible.'

She sighed.

'You heard him, Doctor. It has to be what he wants. It's all that's left for me to do for him…respect his wishes.'

As they stood together on the pavement outside the house before going to their cars, Rowan said grimly, 'I hope that neither of us has anything else like that to deal with today.'

'Don't bank on it,' Davina replied soberly. 'One awful situation often triggers off another.'

'Yes, I know,' he agreed. 'I think you being there helped. It's grim when the bearer of bad tidings is a stranger.'

One day soon Davina was going to discover that he had tidings for her and whether she would see them as good, bad or indifferent, he didn't know.

They arrived back at the practice simultaneously, just as Megan Thompson was coming in for supplies. As they came face to face with the elderly district nurse on the surgery forecourt, Davina hid a smile.

Rowan had done a pretty good job of charming the staff that morning, but Megan was a different matter. She'd been devoted to Andrew Swinburn for years and would look with a jaundiced eye on anyone replacing him.

But as Davina introduced them it was as if he sensed that here was someone to be won over, a hard nut to be cracked, and after the first few moments of frosty-faced wariness Megan thawed out in the warmth of his greeting.

When she'd left them to go about her business he said, 'I saw you smiling. What was that all about?'

'I never thought I'd live to see the day when Megan would welcome a...'

She paused and he said, 'City smoothie into the practice?'

'So you heard what Jack Morrison said. I hoped that you hadn't.'

'Yes, I heard what 'country boy' said.'

'City smoothie, country boy!' she exclaimed. 'That's individual opinions being bandied about. I wonder what label you've given me.'

'You might be surprised if I told you,' he said easily.

'Surprise me, then.'

He was smiling but it didn't reach his eyes. They were cool and guarded.

'Dr D.? The honey of Heatherlea? Vina of the valley?'

Davina had gone pale. Her eyes looked big in her face. It had been just a bit of teasing but he'd scored a hit.

'Where did you get that from?' she asked in a low voice. 'The only person who ever called me Vina was my mother.'

Rowan shrugged. 'Don't know. I come from a family of abbreviators. They call me Row for short.'

It wasn't true but he had to say something, having thrown out the bait and now wishing he hadn't.

The decorator had come downstairs to have a word with him and the conversation came to a halt as the two men discussed colours and styles. As the afternoon asthma clinic was due to start in an hour, Davina went home for a quick lunch.

Going back to the house at midday wasn't normal procedure. She usually had a sandwich on the job, but today she wanted to unwind, to get away from Rowan for a while. It had been an interesting morning and, no doubt, the rest of the day would turn out to be the same, with the dark-eyed stranger feeling his way around.

She still couldn't get over him calling her Vina. It having been her mother's pet name for her, it went without saying that her father had never used it, and Aunt Grace had too much concern for her niece's feelings to remind her of the mother who was no longer there, but for some reason Rowan had latched onto it.

When she got back he said, 'Where've you been, Davina?'

He'd been wondering if he'd upset her with the name from the past and if she'd wanted to get away from him. Yet it hadn't been deliberate. He hadn't known it had been her mother's name for her.

'I went home for some lunch.'

'I see. Is that usual?'

She stared at him with mutinous blue eyes. Surely he didn't object to her having a lunch-hour.

'No. It isn't usual,' she said evenly, unaware of the thoughts coursing through his mind. Telling a lie, she went on to say, 'I wanted to see if there was any message from my aunt. I didn't hear from her over the weekend.'

'And you're concerned?'

'Not exactly.'

She wasn't concerned at all. Grace was having the time of her life and she was well able to look after herself, but she didn't want Rowan to know that he was having a strange effect on her.

Seeing him alongside Jack Morrison had made her realise how few men of his calibre she'd met, and she didn't want it to be like that. A good working relationship demanded trust and impartiality. She could guarantee the first but wasn't too sure she would be able to keep to the second.

And why the inquisition about where she'd been for the last half-hour? She hoped he wasn't going to be keeping tabs on her all the time.

At the end of the working day she was more tired than usual and knew it was the result of tension rather than exertion. She and Andrew had jogged along harmoniously and she'd always felt relaxed with him around, but the new doctor was something else.

He may have had a disturbed night but *he* wasn't flagging as they saw the last patient off the premises in the early evening. In fact, he sounded as if he was in the mood for prolonging the day when he suggested, 'Do you fancy coming up to my de luxe apartment for a drink to celebrate our first day as a team? I think I have a bottle of wine somewhere amongst my still unpacked belongings.'

Surprised at the invitation, Davina hesitated for a moment and then said, 'Er…yes. That would be nice.'

When they went upstairs and he pushed open the door of the apartment, her eyes widened. The decorators had finished for the day but it was clear they'd been putting in some hard work while they'd been there. The green-washed walls had been replaced with pale gold and the woodwork given a first coat of satin-finish cream paint.

As she looked down there were bare floor boards beneath her feet and he said, 'Yes, it's gone. I took the old carpet to the local refuse tip early this morning before surgery. I've got someone coming round later this evening with carpet samples to choose from. What colour would you think to go with these walls?'

'Dark gold or a very delicate green,' she said immediately.

He nodded.

'Hmm. I'd thought of something like that myself.'

Davina was looking around her and she said, 'The rooms up here are large and airy. It has lots of potential.'

'Not as large as the rooms in that big old house of yours, I'll bet,' he countered. 'Maybe you'll show me round some time. It looks very imposing from the outside.'

'You only saw it in the dark,' she said, surprised at his interest.

'Yes, I did, and I imagine it's even more impressive in the light of day.'

'There are stables adjoining,' she told him, 'but they were sold when my father died and the money has been put in a trust until such time as I want to buy into a practice.'

'What was he like, your father?' he asked, and her surprise increased.

'Honourable, hard-working. A man who kept his thoughts to himself and everyone else at arm's length. His wasn't exactly a pleasing personality but I suppose he cared for me in his own way. Not that he would have ever said so.'

The miserable old blighter, Rowan thought. Two beautiful women in his life and he hadn't made either of them happy. Because she *was* beautiful, this young doctor who had come down from the hill on his first day in the village to invite him to breakfast.

But if his mind was on her background, Davina's wasn't. She was eyeing the dusty floorboards that the removal of the carpet had revealed and suggesting, 'I'll give the floor a wash for you if you've got a mop and bucket anywhere to hand.'

Rowan shook his head.

'Not in those smart clothes you've been wearing for the surgery. I'll give the floor a good scrubbing later, but there is something you can do for me.'

'And what's that?'

'Come late shopping with me one night this week to buy some curtains. That's something I'm not looking forward to.'

'I'd love to,' she said enthusiastically. 'By then you'll have chosen carpets, I suppose, so we'll know what we have to match up with.'

Rowan was bending over a packing case and when he straightened up he was holding a bottle of wine.

'I said I had a bottle somewhere, didn't I?' he said triumphantly. 'All we need now are two glasses and I think I know where to put my hand on them.'

As they drank the wine, only inches away from each other on a smart sofa that he'd brought with him, Davina felt suddenly awkward. She was very conscious of his nearness. Her eyes were on the hand nearest to her, holding the glass. It looked strong and capable, like its owner.

What would it be like to be caressed by it? she wondered, and felt her cheeks start to burn at the thought. You're crazy, she told herself. Just because Rowan Westlake is in a class of his own when it comes to attractive men, you don't have to go all dithery. You've got to work with the guy, for heaven's sake.

She got to her feet. 'I must be going, Rowan. Thanks for the drink…and if there is anything at all I can do to help you settle in, do let me know. This room will look lovely once you've got it how you want it.'

He rose to stand beside her and she didn't know if it was the wine or his nearness that was making her feel weak.

'So we're all right for the curtain-choosing?' he asked.

'Yes,' she said, moving away. 'Just let me know which night you want to go.'

As Davina drove home in the spring night, the Land Rover from the Morrison farm fell in behind her and Davina thought that Jack Morrison twice in one day was a bit too much.

When she pulled up in front of Heatherlea he stopped beside her and, winding the window down, said, 'Are you going to invite me in for a drink?'

'No. I'm not,' she told him.

'Why?'

'Because you get too forward.'

'Huh, and what about the new doctor? I saw you up there with him.'

'So?'

'So you haven't known him five minutes and you're drinking with him in his bedroom.'

'Lounge, if you don't mind,' she said coldly, 'and what has it got to do with you? You've already poked your nose in once today.'

'Suit yourself,' he said huffily. 'I've been told that the women in your family are inclined to be free and easy.'

Her eyes were glacial in a white face as she said, 'You're jealous and there is no need to be. I have to work with the man, for heaven's sake. Would I be judging you if I saw you with a new female farmworker? You and I were finished weeks ago. You're as fresh as a basket of whelks and now, if you'll excuse me, I'm going to have my meal. I've been on the go since seven o'clock this morning and I'm ready to unwind, which isn't going to happen with you around.'

Jack switched on the Land Rover's engine.

'OK. I'm off. There are plenty of other fish in the sea.'

Davina sighed.

'You're only peeved because another man has appeared on the scene. You weren't bothered about us splitting up before. Whether you like it or not, Rowan Westlake is here to stay in the valley, and as far as I'm concerned we're just two doctors treating the sick in the neighbourhood.'

What was the matter with him? she thought as he drove away. Rowan had hardly got his foot in the doorway of the practice but already the local talent was getting edgy.

Jack's snide remark about her mother had hurt but there'd been no way she'd take him up on it. That kind of thing she put down to the man's ignorance, but he'd said something else that had hit home.

He'd said that on very short acquaintance she was showing a lot of interest in the new doctor, and she'd been thinking the same thing herself. She could feel her face burning. Maybe Jack was right.

Davina and Rowan went late night shopping in the neighbouring town on Thursday night and, remembering Jack's comments, Davina kept to her surgery manner, rather than treating the shopping spree as a social occasion.

As they walked around the fabric section of the largest store, she found Rowan's glance on her a few times. Eventually he said, 'Are you sure you don't mind giving up your evening?'

'I don't mind at all,' she told him with a smile, feeling that perhaps she'd overdone the restrained manner. 'I love doing this sort of thing. I just don't want you to feel that I'm pushing myself...overpowering you with my presence.'

She might have something there, he thought whimsically. He *was* overpowered by her. Overpowered by the knowledge of who she was, by her attractions, her youthful dedication and her willingness to give up her free time for his benefit.

But he was serious as he turned to face her. 'Nothing of the kind, Davina. You've made this move of mine much more pleasant and interesting than I imagined it would be. I'm indebted to you.'

'So let's do what we're here for,' she said with eyes sparkling as she guided him to a counter where attractive curtaining was on display.

They chose a colour that was between the pale yellow of the walls and the deeper gold of the carpet and as they came away with the promise that the ready-mades would be delivered the next day, Rowan said, 'Let's go and eat. I don't know about you but I'm starving.'

The store had its own restaurant and, having no wish to travel further after a long day at the practice, they found a table and proceeded to serve themselves from an appetising display.

He ate with purpose and pleasure and as she watched him Davina couldn't believe that it was happening. A week ago she hadn't even known this man and now he was slotted into her life as firmly as the ground beneath her feet.

They'd left her car back at the practice and when he drove her there to collect it he said, 'Thanks again, Davina. I hope I can return the favour some time.'

'It was a pleasure,' she told him, and was amazed how much she meant it.

CHAPTER THREE

DAVINA had enjoyed working with Andrew, but with Rowan's take-over of the practice, job satisfaction had taken on a new meaning. As the days went by she discovered that not only was he a very competent doctor, his organising skills were formidable.

The decorators had moved downstairs now and the surgery area was being transformed, like the apartment above. It meant working amongst ladders and pots of paint, but most of the work was done in the evenings and at weekends to avoid disruption as much as possible, and as the previous sombre decor disappeared new furnishings began to appear.

She had been in the apartment once since the night they'd shared the bottle of wine. Rowan had invited her up one day at the end of morning surgery to see the finished project, and as she'd observed the changes she'd said enviously. 'I'd love a place like this. You've transformed it. Apart from the halls of residence when I was at college, I've only ever lived in Heatherlea and sometimes I wish I had a place of my own.

He'd observed her with the keen hazel gaze that was so much a part of him. 'So why not do something about it?'

'It would mean leaving Grace on her own and I wouldn't do that. For years there were three of us then Dad died, and if I were to move out it would leave just one and I know she would feel it.'

'If she loves you, she'll understand,' he'd said, as if that were the matter closed.

For some reason Davina felt challenged and said abruptly, 'Grace *does* love me. She's the only person in my life whose love I can be sure of. I could never be sure of my dad's feelings. Probably because I resemble my mother so much. As for her, my mother, well, she left me, didn't she?' Her voice tightened. 'It's easy for you to talk. I had a complicated childhood. Maybe yours was different.'

Rowan turned away and his glance was on the hillside behind the practice where the stone outline of Heatherlea stood out on the skyline.

'It had its twists and turns,' he said flatly, and wondered why he wasn't seizing the opportunity to bring it all out into the open.

One of the receptionists came through on the internal line at that moment to say that there was someone to see him down below, and the discussion ended there, leaving the two doctors with mixed feelings.

Davina was upset because a tour of the refurbished rooms had left them both, all from a chance remark, with an uneasy feeling. Rowan wondered if he was letting his reluctance to damage their relationship affect his better judgement...

The person waiting to see him had turned out to be Clive Holden.

'Hello, Davina, darling,' he said when she followed Rowan downstairs, and she watched Rowan's dark brows rise at the familiarity.

'What can I do for you, Mr Holden?' he said levelly. 'We have met before, I think.'

The other man nodded. 'Sure have. Just call me Clive.' With a meaningful glance in her direction he added, 'But to get down to business. I've been told that you're doing this place up, and now I'm here I see that it is so.'

'And?' Rowan prompted unsmilingly.

'As you will know, I'm in arts and crafts and I'm wondering if I could sell you any paintings or sculptures to accentuate the new look.'

Clive wasn't without cheek, Davina thought irritably, but she supposed he couldn't be blamed for seizing an opportunity that he thought might be there. But he was as bad as Jack when it came to showing off in front of the new doctor. What was the matter with them? Wary of the competition?

They needn't be. Mesmerising though Rowan might be, the chat they'd just had upstairs had shown they'd need to be on each other's wavelength more for anything of that kind to develop.

'I'll think about it,' Rowan said distantly, and Davina wondered what was causing the ice to form—the previous meeting with Clive that time in the newsagent's or his familiarity towards herself. Yet she could hardly see it being that. Rowan had no claim on her other than as his assistant.

'Sure,' Clive said, 'but don't leave it too late. There's a big demand for my stuff.'

As if! she thought as he made his departure with a nod and a wink in her direction.

'You seem to be on good terms with all the male yokels,' Rowan commented when Clive had gone.

Still out of tune with him, she snapped back, 'Locals…not yokels. And, yes, I have friends of both sexes in the valley. I *did* have a life before you came.'

And what was he going to make of that? she thought dismally as soon as the words were out. That it had changed since he'd come? Well, it had, hadn't it? Changed so much that everything he said or did mattered.

They separated after that, each to do their home visits, and as he drove out to a remote farm where he'd been asked to call on a woman with multiple sclerosis Rowan was thinking that his annoyance earlier had been a bit misplaced. As Davina had pointed out, it was no business of his who she was friendly with but, for heaven's sake, a woman of her intelligence and education should be turning her attention to someone like himself.

As he caught a glimpse of his set face in the mirror above the dashboard, he knew that it wasn't only her welfare he was concerned about. It wouldn't take much for him to fall head over heels in love for the second time in his life. But there were a couple of reasons why that wouldn't be a good idea.

He'd already had one bad experience in the romance stakes and didn't want another. And more of a deterrent even than that was what he had to do when Davina's Aunt Grace came home. He had to wait until then because his young assistant would need some support when he butted into another part of her life, and from the way she'd described her aunt, Grace would be the best person to give it.

Pamela Sowerby's notes told him that she'd been diagnosed with multiple sclerosis nineteen years previously, and there was nothing in the paperwork to indicate that the illness had progressed much until the last couple of years when it had begun to make its presence felt. Numbness in the lower limbs had been recorded, rigidity, muscle weakness and occasionally slurred speech.

Davina had told Rowan that Pamela was a down-to-earth, positive-thinking woman, and if the future held any fears she hadn't as yet shown it, but today when he arrived at the small sheep farm he found her in a state of panic.

'I can't see, Doctor,' she cried as her husband led him into a cheerful sitting room. 'The MS seems to be making up for lost time. I was all right for years, but now there isn't a day goes by without some sort of a reminder that it hasn't gone away. I can cope with the rest of it, but not this! My husband and sons need me to look after them and help with the farm, and I can't do it tapping around with a white stick!'

Rowan let her get it off her chest and then said quietly, 'Tell me, have you any vision at all, Mrs Sowerby?'

'Just a little bit in the centre of my eye,' she sobbed.

'Does it hurt when you move your eyes?'

'Yes.'

'And does it feel tender when you touch them?'

'Yes.'

He nodded. 'MS can cause damage to the optic nerve. You're suffering from optic neuritis. That's the bad news. The good news is that, though it may recur, an attack often clears up in about six weeks.'

The distressed woman let out a sigh of relief.

'Thank goodness for that! I can put up with it if it's only temporary.'

His face was grave. 'I can understand your feelings but it may recur in a few months, a year, or even longer than that. But for the present you should get your sight back soon. I'm going to prescribe an anticosteroid drug which should aid the return of vision, but I'm afraid it won't prevent it happening again some time in the future.'

With the promise of a reprieve Pamela was regaining her composure and she said, 'I'm told that Dr Swinburn has gone and you've taken over.'

'Yes, that's right,' he said as he wrote out the prescription.

'And what about Davina Richards? She's one of us, you know. Born and bred in the valley.'

He smiled. Talk about being a member of the clan!

'Nothing has changed as far as Davina is concerned. She's still with the practice for as long as she wants to be.'

'Good.' She turned to her husband who'd been edging towards the door as soon as his wife had perked up. 'Put the kettle on, George, and make the doctor a brew.'

Rowan shook his head.

'I'm sure that your husband has more important things to do than make cups of tea for me, Mrs Sowerby. I'll be on my way. I shall want to see you again next week to see how your vision is progressing. If you can't make it to the surgery, I'll visit.' And with a smile for the harassed-looking farmer he left them to their day.

As he pulled out of the hill road and joined the traffic going towards the village Rowan was thinking about what he'd said to Pamela Sowerby. It was true. Davina would be welcome as part of the practice for as long as she wanted to be. He was lucky to have her services. She still had a lot to learn, but when she didn't know she would ask, and when she did know she put the knowledge into practice efficiently and without fuss.

He awoke each morning with pleasure inside him because she would be part of his day. If he had any misgivings about *his* future role in her life, he put them to one side because he wanted nothing to interfere with these first few weeks of busy contentment.

When his mobile rang he pulled over to the side of the road to answer it, and it was her voice on the line.

'John Warrender, the lung-cancer patient, died suddenly a few moments ago,' she said soberly. 'His wife has just rung the practice. Are you anywhere near their place?'

'Yes. I'll go right there,' he told her. 'Or do you think they would prefer that you went? After all, they know you better than they know me and sometimes a familiar face is more comforting than a strange one at such times.'

'Why don't I meet you there?' she suggested. 'I've finished my rounds and can be there in a quarter of an hour.'

'Yes. Good idea. I'm on my way,' Rowan replied.

They arrived within minutes of each other and the dead man's wife collapsed weeping in Davina's arms when she saw her. As the young doctor stroked her hair she said gently, 'Be glad for him, Angie. No more pain. No more trying to fight a lost cause. John died at home, which was how he wanted it to be. It's just a shell lying there. His spirit will even now be soaring to freedom.'

Rowan was signing the death certificate and he felt his chest tighten. Davina was only young. Yet there was a depth to her not found in many. He'd faced up to the finality of death himself not long ago. It had made all the earthly things he valued seem unimportant and had been an event that had triggered off something he'd never expected having to deal with.

As they went to their cars, leaving a calmer Angie Warrender to wait for the undertaker, Rowan said, 'People in our profession can become so accustomed to death they become immune to it. I'm glad I asked you to join me. You were just what that poor woman needed.'

Davina smiled. The harmony between them was back and that was how she wanted it to be. In the midst of the grief that came with death, and the satisfaction to be derived from healing, they were a team.

Rowan had walked into her life and it was as if he'd always been there. She was falling in love for the first time and as she met his glance he said, 'What? What are you thinking?'

'That we seem to be getting on very well,' she replied cautiously.

It was his turn to smile but as on another occasion it didn't reach his eyes.

'Don't tempt providence,' he warned. 'It's when things are going well that trouble is usually just round the corner. I know. I've been there.'

'And what does that mean?'

He wasn't to be drawn. Getting into his car, he said, 'I'll see you back at the practice. We should just about have time for a bite before the antenatal clinic starts.'

It was clear that romance wasn't on *his* mind, she thought as she switched on the engine, but there was time. All the time in the world for them to get to know each other.

When the early evening surgery was over Davina walked out into a balmy May night and Rowan's voice said from behind her, 'Have you anything planned for this evening?'

'No. Why?'

'I thought we might eat at the pub and then perhaps you could show me round the village. I don't see much of it when I'm in the car and I seem to remember you once telling me that it has its ghosts and legends.'

It had been a long and tiring day but her exhaustion fell away at his suggestion. A walk along the valley with him would make a pleasant change from the things they usually did together, such as discussing patients' notes and checking the progress of pregnant mums-to-be. They hadn't really been alone, away from practice matters, since the night they'd gone to choose the curtains for the apartment.

It was a pity she couldn't dash home to change into something more glamorous than the smart navy suit she'd worn at the practice. Though maybe she could. It would only take a matter of minutes. When she suggested it, Rowan said, 'Why don't we both do that? I feel as if I've been wearing this shirt and tie for ever. I'll meet you at the pub shortly.'

When she returned, dressed in a short blue denim jacket, white jeans and shoes with raised soles that brought her up to his height, Davina knew it had been worth the effort.

'We should do this more often,' he murmured, with his glance on the soft curve of her throat.

Her blood was warming. Had he any idea how she was drawn to him? In that moment the practice was a million miles away. Infections and infarctions, haemorrhoids and liver damage belonged to another life. All that mattered was a magic moment in a summer night.

She could feel his gaze on her all the time they were eating and once they'd finished he said, 'So, shall we stroll the night away, Davina?'

'Yes, why not?' she breathed, and hoped he couldn't hear her heart thudding in her breast.

As they walked towards the dark stone church that had looked down on the valley for centuries Rowan said, 'The feeling of ancient lore is strong around here. I can imagine warring tribes fighting it out in bygone days and in later years the gentry lording it over the peasants.'

'There was once a yeoman from this valley who envied the rich in their fine clothes and carriages and vowed to make something of himself,' she said. 'He left his humble beginnings behind and went to London from where he never looked back. Through hard work and determination he became a member of the Goldsmiths' Society, eventually becoming jeweller to King Edward IV. He held the position under four successive kings and in 1482 was made Lord Mayor of London.'

'I am impressed. But are you sure you're not getting him mixed up with Dick Whittington?' he teased. 'Or was it he who inspired the lad who went to London and found the streets paved with gold?'

'The story is true,' she told him, 'You'll find it in the history books.'

'You love this place that's always been your home, don't you?' he said solemnly.

She shrugged slim shoulders inside the denim jacket and with her colour rising told him, 'Yes, I do, but people matter more than places, don't they?'

They were on the hill road now. Soon Heatherlea would be in sight and what then? she wondered. Should she ask him in? She knew that the house interested him, though she wasn't sure why. But she didn't want Rowan in her home because of its architecture. She wanted him there because he wanted to be where she was.

They were feet apart, yet she felt as if they were touching, so aware was she of him. When she gave a quick sideways glance she found his dark gaze upon her.

'What are you thinking?' he asked softly.

Feeling suddenly reckless, she said, 'I'm thinking that I'm falling in love with you, and I'm not sure whether it's a good idea.'

He reached out and took her hand, pulling her towards him as he did so. 'You're wise to question the sense of it,' he told her as she stood in the circle of his arms.

'Love doesn't come with guidelines, Davina. It's all yearnings and urges that put common sense to flight.'

'And do I take it that you're not in the market for it?'

With his mouth against her brow he murmured, 'There's nothing I'd like more than to make love to you at this very moment, but it isn't that simple.'

She was stiffening in his arms.

'Why? Do you want me to make an appointment first?'

'That's crazy talk. Let me explain.' But she was wrenching herself out of his arms and marching off up the path like an express train. How could he be so clinical about something as magical as falling in love? she thought as she flung back the garden gate and fished in her pocket for a key.

He was behind her and he swung her round, gripping her forearms, 'You're going to listen whether you like it or not, Davina,' he said tightly. 'There's something you need to know about me. I should have seen this coming and told you before.'

'Told me what?' she cried, but he didn't reply.

They were no longer alone in the summer night. A taxi was pulling up behind them, and as the door opened Davina saw a familiar figure smiling at her.

'Surprise! Surprise! I'm home, Davina.' Throwing off Rowan's hold for the second time, she ran to greet the plump, grey-haired woman stepping out of the taxi.

'Aunt Grace!' she cried. 'Why didn't you let me know you were coming home?'

As the two women hugged each other joyfully Grace said, 'Like I said, I wanted to surprise you.' She looked over her niece's shoulder at Rowan, who was thinking grimly that this could be the moment of reckoning whether he wanted it to be or not. 'Are you going to introduce me?'

If she recognised the name, that would be it, he thought. Grace hadn't been around when it had all been happening. She'd appeared on the scene later, but it was a name that would have been bandied about at that time.

When he'd introduced himself to Davina she'd shown no signs of recognition, so he'd accepted that she'd never heard it before, but her aunt was a different kettle of fish.

Their tense situation before the taxi had appeared was forgotten in the pleasure of the moment as Davina told her, 'Andrew Swinburn has retired, Aunt Grace. This is Rowan Westlake, who has taken his place.'

He almost groaned out loud as the woman standing by the gate surrounded by luggage said slowly, 'Westlake? That's not a name from around these parts. Are you related to Owen Westlake, by any chance?'

'He was my father,' he told her levelly

'And so what has brought you here? Haven't your family done us enough harm?' she said coldly.

Davina was listening in bewildered amazement. A moment ago everything had been wonderful. But now, as she observed her aunt and Rowan, it was as if they'd been turned to stone.

'What's going on?' she cried. 'What has Rowan's father got to do with us?'

'He was the man that your mother went away with,' Grace told her flatly.

Davina was clinging on to the gate for support as her legs began to sag.

'What? I can't believe it! You came slinking into my life without a word about who you were!' she said accusingly. 'Knowing what your father had done.'

'It takes two to make that kind of bargain, Davina,' he said sombrely. 'Isabel was a willing part of it from what I've been told. I've been waiting for the right moment to tell you who I am. In fact, I was on the point of explaining when your aunt arrived.'

'Explaining!' she cried. 'What is there to explain? That you decided to come and have a nose around at the scene of the crime and get to know the deserted daughter at the same time. You're despicable!'

'This has all gone horribly wrong,' he said grimly. 'I came here because I was asked to. I didn't want to but I had no choice.'

'So why buy the practice?'

'That was pure impulse. I like this part of the world and wanted my own set-up. I thought I'd combine the two projects.'

'Projects! So getting to know me was a ''project'', was it?'

'Look, Davina,' he said evenly. 'You're overwrought. I'll go. Maybe we can talk tomorrow.'

'The only thing I shall want to talk about tomorrow are the conditions of the month's notice that I'm committed to.'

'So you would leave the practice. Deprive the people who know you so well of your services...out of pique?'

'I think that you *had* better go, Dr Westlake,' Grace said. 'Maybe we will all feel calmer tomorrow.'

When Rowan had gone Davina's tears flowed. Pride had helped her to hold them back while he'd been there but now they were pouring down her cheeks.

'I was falling in love with him, Aunt Grace,' she sobbed, 'and he knew it. Knew what he was doing to me, and never said anything. How could he? We're related. He's my stepbrother, for goodness' sake. The son of that man!'

'You're not blood relations,' Grace pointed out in a calmer tone. 'And we've never known if your mother and his father did marry. I doubt your father would ever have agreed to a divorce. There would be nothing legally wrong in you marrying Rowan Westlake...and much as I'm appalled to find him amongst us, virtually on our doorstep, at a first glance he is a very attractive man.'

'Handsome is as handsome does, you've always told me,' Davina said glumly. 'I'd rather have someone who looked like a Neanderthal man and was honest than someone who does that to me.'

'And *are* you going to give in your notice?' her aunt asked. 'Or was it said in the heat of the moment? Be sure you're not cutting off your nose to spite your face.'

'How can I do anything else?' Davina asked dismally. 'I love working amongst the valley folk, but how can I carry on with Rowan around all the time? Knowing who he is and where he comes from. It would have been bad enough if he'd told me who he was at the beginning. But to keep me in the dark like he has is awful.'

Talk about the sins of the fathers being visited on the children, Rowan thought ruefully as he walked back home.

He'd been at boarding school when it had happened and so, like Davina, had been only on the edge of things. In those days he'd stayed with his grandparents during school holidays and overall had seen very little of his widower father.

His mother had died the previous year and from things his grandmother had let slip he'd discovered that his father and Isabel Richards had been very close in their teens but had both married someone else.

It had been when she'd gone to visit her parents that they'd met up again and realised they'd never stopped loving each other. His father had wanted it all out in the open but, knowing the nature of her husband and afraid that she might lose her daughter, Isabel had stuck with Michael Richards until the day he'd found out about the affair.

It was ironic that Rowan had only got to know the full story when his father had been dying. Up to that time he hadn't even known that Isabel Richards had a daughter. His father had never mentioned her. Whether because of pain or guilt he didn't know.

What he had known was that after fleeing from the enraged husband, who had threatened them both with a shotgun, Isabel had pleaded with his father to turn the car round and go back for her daughter.

But, afraid for their lives, he'd refused and in desperation she'd grabbed the steering-wheel to try and make him turn back. They'd crashed into a tree and she'd been killed outright.

Devastated by the loss, his father had worked abroad a lot after that and it was only after he'd retired that they'd become close. Owen Westlake had died from cancer three months previously, and as he'd lay dying he'd made Rowan promise to go and find Isabel's daughter and tell her that her mother hadn't had any intention of leaving her behind. That she'd been killed because of that determination. That she really loved her child.

Rowan had been appalled.

'It's a bit late, Dad, isn't it?' he protested. 'Twenty years ago, to be exact. Wouldn't it be better to let sleeping dogs lie?'

The sick man shook his head emphatically.

'I can't go with it on my conscience that I never went to tell her about her mother's death. As far as I know, Richards was never aware of it. He'd have been round to gloat if he had been. Rubbing it in that it had done me no good, taking her from him. I saw to the funeral and the story of the accident never got into the papers. The folks in the area where they lived wouldn't have known about it, either, as the accident occurred over a hundred miles away from her home. I suppose I owed it to Richards to tell him, but he'd already threatened to shoot me, and he'd never really loved Isabel. She was just a possession not to be taken away.

'So will you do this one last thing for me, Rowan?' he pleaded, and even though he cringed at the thought of what his father was asking of him, he hadn't been able to refuse.

Taking over the practice in the valley was a spur-of-the-moment decision, as he'd tried to explain to Davina, and the last thing he'd ever expected to happen had been that he should find himself working with the desirable, long-legged blonde who was Isabel Richard's daughter. The memory of seeing her looking down on him from horseback as she'd introduced herself was still crystal clear.

If he'd had any brains he should have told her then. Got it off his chest and been done with it. But deep down inside him there'd been a reluctance to intrude into her life. And look where it had got him.

He supposed that some people would say she should be grateful to him for bringing the tidings that her mother had never intended to leave her behind. But that message had to walk hand in hand with the news that Isabel had lived only a few hours after her flight from the valley. That she'd been dead for a very long time.

So far Davina was still uninformed of the most important things she needed to know. All that she was aware of at that moment was his identity, and she'd discovered that in the most hurtful way possible.

What next? he thought. He couldn't force her to listen to what he had to tell her. He'd already upset her enough. Would she turn up for surgery in the morning? He prayed that she would. If she was on the premises he would at least be near her, whether she still refused to talk to him or not.

He could imagine her chagrin at having told him she was falling in love with him and being repulsed. That would have been bad enough, but to find out who it was that she was falling in love with would have been the final straw.

What it boiled down to was that he and Davina were the innocent pawns from the backwash of long ago. Yet he didn't regret coming to the valley. If he hadn't agreed to carry out his father's wishes, he would never have met her. Whatever the future held, he wouldn't have wanted to miss that.

CHAPTER FOUR

WHEN Rowan picked up the post from behind the surgery door the next morning there was an expensive-looking envelope amongst it addressed in a familiar flamboyant hand.

He groaned. Carlotta! What did she want? They'd been engaged once, he and Carlotta Germaine, and whenever he thought about it he didn't understand what had possessed him to become involved with her. They were as different as chalk from cheese.

The sultry actress had been in a show that he'd gone to see with a friend who'd been acquainted with her, and when they'd been introduced a heady relationship had come out of it.

She was talented, very ambitious and came from a totally different world to himself. It had been a brief attraction of opposites. The dedicated doctor with the charismatic aura of the medicine man about him and the actress from the fascinating world of the theatre.

They'd become engaged and had been talking of marriage when he'd discovered that she'd been sleeping with the director of her current show, and he'd come down to earth with a bump.

She must have got his address from his previous practice, he thought angrily. They had no right to have given it to her. But he knew Carlotta. She could charm the birds out of the trees if she chose to.

'Darling Rowan,' she'd written. 'Am doing a summer show at one of the Manchester theatres. If you check the

entertainment advertisements you'll see my name, virtually up in lights. Can't we let bygones be bygones and
meet up somewhere? I could send you free tickets. Will
ring you. I have your number.'

His face was grim. If there was one person he didn't
want in his life at that moment, or any other time for that
matter, it was Carlotta. She could ring him until she was
blue in the face and it would make no difference, just as
long as she didn't take it into her head to come to the
practice.

But he had more important things on his mind than an
ex-fiancée and as time for morning surgery drew near he
found himself watching the clock. When Davina's car
pulled up on the forecourt he breathed a sigh of relief.

It was one step in the right direction. At least she'd
arrived. After last night he'd doubted whether she would
show up. But his relief dwindled as she made her way
straight to the office of the recently appointed practice
manager without a glance in his direction.

She was checking on her notice requirements, he
thought dismally, so she hadn't changed her mind.

'I was hoping you'd had a rethink,' he said quietly
when she came out, 'but you're obviously still intending
to leave.'

She smiled but there was something brittle about it that
he didn't like.

'If you must know,' she said with the smile still in
evidence, 'I've been arranging a holiday.'

'I see.' He could feel his jaw dropping but was damned
if he was going to let her see she'd rattled him. 'So
you've changed your mind about leaving.'

'Yes. Why should I be driven out of the practice because you play around with the truth?'

'Driven!' he exclaimed. 'No one is driving you anywhere, Davina. Leaving was your idea, not mine. And keeping silent about a distressing matter is not "playing with the truth". It might be classed as avoiding it, but not distorting it. And my reluctance to come clean was for both our sakes.'

'With regard to arranging holidays,' he went on, 'I'm the person you're supposed to consult, as you well know. If you're staying on we have to make sure that absence on either of our parts is convenient for the other, and for the practice in general. When do you want to go?'

'Tomorrow.'

'I see. You're not wasting any time in getting away from me. Where are you planning on going?'

'I haven't decided.'

'So I'm right. You just want to get away from me.'

'Correct.'

'All right. Take the time off. I'll manage. And when you come back we have to talk. There are things you need to know.'

'Wrong!' she said coldly. 'If you're going to dig up the past to justify that father of yours, save your breath. We're lumbered with each other here at the practice, but that doesn't mean we have to be in each other's company apart from that.' And without giving him time to answer, she went to the door of the waiting room and called in the first patient of the day.

So much for that, Rowan thought. He'd known last night it wasn't going to be easy. Her aunt's unexpected return had really shown him up in a bad light. He hadn't expected to be as welcome as the flowers in spring when he identified himself, but the way it had happened had made it a lot worse and Davina's manner this morning was proof of that...

*   *   *

Mingled with Davina's hurt amazement at discovering Rowan's identity was sadness that her mother's betrayal was being brought into focus again after such a long time and she didn't understand why. Why he'd come to the valley for one thing. Owen Westlake's son of all people. If it was out of cruel curiosity she couldn't bear it.

As she'd tossed and turned during the night hours she'd kept telling herself bitterly that he probably saw it as some sort of joke. History repeating itself. Isabel Richards's daughter falling for the son of the man who'd enticed her away from her family.

And now, facing up to a busy day at the surgery, she was still numb with shock. Had Rowan been banking on Grace not recognising the name? she wondered. If he had it had been a vain hope. Her aunt was nobody's fool. She wouldn't have forgotten. As for herself she'd never heard the name before. Grace had protected her from what had gone on and most of it had washed over her.

She'd cried for her mother and been frightened of her father's rage, but she'd been too young for the rest of it to register. How much did Rowan know? she wondered. He would have been in his early teens at that time and probably still mourning the loss of his own mother. She'd heard it said that Owen Westlake had been recently bereaved when he and her mother had met up again.

You've had a lucky escape, she'd told herself in the first light of a summer dawn. Rowan Westlake is the last person you should be falling in love with. If you don't watch it you're going to be as unlucky in love as your mother was.

But wasn't it too late already? She wasn't falling in love with him. She had already fallen. For good or bad she was in love with Rowan Westlake and after what had happened last night she felt with a dismal certainty that nothing was going to come of it.

He was the last person she would have expected to deceive her. His apparent integrity had been one of the things that had drawn her to him. That and his vitality…and the sexual awareness that he aroused in her.

As she'd huddled beneath the bed covers her face had burned as she'd recalled the moment when she'd admitted that she was falling in love with him. She'd been in his arms at the time, but it hadn't done her much good as he'd immediately started trying to salve a guilty conscience by saying he had something to tell her. But would she have ever got to know who he was if Grace hadn't turned up?

Those moments beside the garden gate with her aunt's luggage strewn around and the cab driver patiently waiting to be paid had turned from joy to stunned hurt and she felt as if nothing would ever be the same again.

As the patients came and went with their assorted ailments, ranging from a vasectomy request to a verruca, Davina kept her mind strictly on the job. She was taking two weeks off starting tomorrow and hadn't a clue how she was going to spend the time, but for today it was business as usual.

The time off was at short notice and not really fair to Rowan but she didn't care. He would have seen a lot of her mother over the years and she'd seen nothing. Where was the justice in that…

Had Isabel sent him to pave the way for a reunion or something similar she kept asking herself. If she had it would be the cruellest thing of all to send her stepson instead of coming herself.

Yet she wasn't going to find out anything if she didn't let him say what he had to say. But she could live with that. He'd appeared in her life and she'd welcomed him with open arms, having no idea that he had a hidden agenda, and now she wanted nothing else to do with him.

When she went to consult Rowan at lunchtime about a patient she'd seen during the morning, Lucy the practice nurse, said, 'Dr Westlake has gone up to his apartment.'

Davina hesitated. She didn't want to go up there and be alone with him, but she had her home visits to do and a hospital appointment to make for the patient in question, so it looked as if she had no choice.

When he opened the door to her Rowan gave a twisted smile. 'Taking a chance, aren't you?' he said. 'Visiting the villain in his den. Do I take it that you've come to tell me you're prepared to listen to what I have to say?'

'No. You don't. I'm here to ask your advice about a patient.'

He stepped back. 'You'd better come in, then.' She perched on the edge of the nearest chair. 'So, what's the problem?'

She sighed. What would he say if she were to tell him that 'the problem' was that she was angry and confused, hurt and bewildered, and she wanted it all to go away so that they could be as they'd been before?

But life wasn't like that. Once trust had gone from a relationship there wasn't much left to salvage. In the last twenty-four hours her life had been turned upside down and the dark hazel gaze of the man in front of her told her that he was reading her mind. Yet he was making no attempt to offer comfort.

'You said you have a problem with a patient,' he reminded her. 'Are you going to tell me what it is, or are we going to spend the rest of the afternoon in silent contemplation?'

The sarcasm brought her thoughts back in line and there was enough anger amongst them to bring her to her feet like a rocket.

'Don't speak to me like that,' she stormed. 'I'm not here to be patronised. If *you've* soon got over last night's upset, *I* haven't.'

'So that's what you think, is it, Davina?' he said levelly. 'That I'm happy to be seen as something lower than the ground beneath your feet? That goes to show that you don't know me as well as you think you do.'

'That's just it!' she cried. 'I don't know you at all. You're part of the miserable past and I think you should go.'

'What? I'm not going anywhere. I've sunk a lot of time and money into this place and I'm staying. I had no part in what happened long ago and neither did you, so why should we have to suffer for it now?'

'Because your coming here has raked it all up again. I'm amazed that some of the older folk here in the valley haven't latched on to who you are.'

'Does it matter?'

'Yes, it does. There are a thousand other places where you could have established yourself in a practice, but you chose here.'

'Maybe it was destiny, Davina,' he said, his voice softening, and he took a step towards her. 'You've no idea how beautiful you are with those sapphire eyes sparking blue fire.' He took another step, and another, and when they were almost touching he murmured, 'We can't go on like this. Daggers drawn and hurting. I'm here now, here to stay, and nothing is going to change that.'

He reached out and cupped her face between his hands and as her senses sprang to life at his touch Davina was amazed that their anger could change to desire so quickly.

When he kissed her it was as if nothing else mattered but his mouth on hers. Like stepping out of a stormy sea on to a safe and delightful shore. She could have stayed there for ever, letting her heart rule her head, but the moment was about to be broken into.

'Oh! Sorry! Am I breaking into something?' a voice said from behind them in the open doorway, and when Davina raised her head and looked over Rowan's shoulders she saw a sultry-looking, dark-haired woman observing them.

'Carlotta!' Rowan sighed, without turning his head. 'You haven't wasted any time. I only got your letter this morning.'

As Davina eased herself out of his arms the newcomer laughed huskily and to the young doctor it sounded like a caress.

'You know me, Rowan. I strike while the iron is hot.'

'I'll speak to you later about the patient, Dr Westlake,' Davina said quickly, with a desperate urge to be somewhere else before he felt compelled to introduce her to the exotic bird-of-prey type that had just arrived.

'Yes, sure, Davina,' he said absently, as if for once he was out of his depth, but the moment she'd gone he was back on form.

'What do you want from me, Carlotta?' he asked coolly. 'Are you between affairs and thought you'd have a stir at the old porridge?'

'You were never that stodgy,' she gurgled. 'In fact, I've often wished we hadn't broken up.'

'Your memory must be failing,' he said in the same cool tone. 'You had no choice in the matter, if you remember. There was nothing mutual about it.'

Full red lips were drawn back.

'And now you've found yourself someone else. The young blonde who's just made a quick departure.'

'Davina is a doctor working alongside me in the practice.'

'Really? Who would have thought it? So was that some kind of therapy you were trying out?'

'Don't try being smart with me, Carlotta. It doesn't work, as you found out. And now I have some house calls to make. I don't know why you came. Whatever the reason, I don't want to know.'

The red lips were pouting now. 'I came for old times' sake and to bring you this,' she said, placing a theatre ticket on a nearby table.

'Yes. I'm sure you did.'

He was picking up his case and holding the doorhandle ready to lock up behind them.

'All right. I get the message,' she said. 'If you don't want the ticket, give it to one of the peasants. I imagine that the folks round here don't get much culture. Whatever possessed you to come to such a place?'

He could imagine Davina's expression if she heard that, he thought wryly. Unable to resist the opportunity, he said, 'Centuries ago one of the ''peasants'' from this place became Lord Mayor of London, and since when has any production you've been involved in been classed as ''culture''?'

'Where can I get something to eat?' she asked, as if she hadn't heard him.

'The pub,' he said briefly as she preceded him down the stairs.

When she appeared in the reception area all eyes were upon her, and as she went swaying through the outer doors Rowan gave an exasperated groan and went to find

Davina, wondering as he did so if there was a curse on him.

Nothing was going right between Davina and himself. It had been for a few moments upstairs but then she had appeared. He'd thought she might, but not so soon. What game was she playing? he wondered. Whatever it was, he felt sure that it had been enough for his young assistant to get the impression that Carlotta had some sort of claim on him. And there was nothing less true than that.

Lucy and Megan were doing smear tests, and when the younger of the two women saw him looking for Davina she said, 'Dr Richards has gone to do her house calls, Dr Westlake. She needs to make a hospital appointment for Mr Jackson from the post office but wants a word with you first. Can you call her on her mobile?'

'I'm sorry about what happened earlier,' he said the moment she answered his call. 'Carlotta Germaine and I were once engaged and she thinks it gives her the right to butt into my life whenever she feels like it.'

'You don't have to explain to me,' she replied. 'She did me a favour. For a few seconds I'd forgotten that you're my stepbrother, and a devious one at that.'

'I...am...not...your...stepbrother,' he said slowly. 'For one thing your father would have never agreed to a divorce, and for another something else happened to prevent my father and Isabel marrying. So don't let that be a reason for avoiding me, Davina.'

Once again the opportunity was there to tell her that her mother was dead but he couldn't do it over the phone. It would be too cruel. He needed to be there when he told her. Whether she would want him to be was another matter, but he had to be just in case.

'I don't want to talk about them,' she was saying.

'They've kept me out of their lives all these years and that's how it can stay.'

He opened his mouth to reason with her and then thought better of it. Once again the needs of a patient were being put to one side and it wouldn't do.

'All right. Have it your own way,' he said dismissively. 'Let's get down to the problem you have with Bob Jackson.'

'I suspect he may have stomach cancer and am not sure whether I should send him to Christies or to see the stomach specialist at the Infirmary.'

'I'd send him to see the fellow at the Infirmary first,' he advised. 'He'll make a diagnosis and if you're right will either operate or pass him on to Christies himself. OK?'

'Yes. That's all I needed to know. Bye for now.' And without giving him time to say anything further, she rang off.

When Davina had finished her rounds she stopped off at the post office to let the postmaster know the details of his appointment, and as she was leaving she saw the woman who had walked in on her brief moment of enchantment with Rowan.

Carlotta Germaine was getting into a car on the forecourt of the village pub, but when she saw Davina she changed her mind and came strolling across.

'Hi, there,' she said. 'Rowan tells me that you're a doctor, too.' Davina nodded mutely. 'He and I used to be engaged and I thought I'd look him up for old times' sake. Do I take it that you and he have something going?'

She was smiling and Davina wondered how genuine it was.

'Yes…er…no,' she said hesitantly, taken aback by the directness of the question. 'What you saw was just…'

Carlotta placed a hand heavy with rings on Davina's arm and with the smile still in place told her, 'It's all right. Rowan has made it quite plain that he doesn't want anything more to do with me. I was a fool. Behaved badly and now wish I hadn't. Men like him don't come along very often.'

'How long have you known him?' Davina asked. Maybe this colourful brunette had met his family. Maybe she could tell her something about them. Where she couldn't stand to hear it from him, she could cope with hearing it from someone else.

'I met him a year ago. We got engaged within three months and he broke it off a few weeks later because he didn't approve of my sleeping habits.'

'Did you ever meet his family?'

It was a sneaky way of finding answers to the questions that plagued her mind, but she couldn't resist asking.

'I met his father once briefly. He wasn't very well at the time, but was a handsome man and most charming. Must have been a stunner when he was younger, and Rowan is very much like him.'

Wonderful! Davina thought. Not only was he Owen Westlake's son but he was made in his image.

'And his mother…er, stepmother?' she probed.

Carlotta was observing her curiously.

'Why do you ask?' When no answer was forthcoming, she went on. 'His mother died when he was in his early teens, so I was told, and there was no other woman in the house.'

So the romance hadn't lasted, Davina thought numbly. Rowan had said that Owen and her mother had never married, and that must have been what he'd meant. So where was she? Why hadn't she come home? The answer came on the heels of the question. Isabel had known that Michael Richards would never have her back.

'I suppose you have some reason for asking,' Carlotta was saying, 'and if it's because you're worried about meeting his parents, you have your answer...no mother and a poorly father. And now I have to go. I'm in a show in Manchester and have to get back for tonight's performance.'

So it had been a case of the actress and the doctor, Davina thought as Carlotta's car sped off in the summer afternoon. A meeting of fact and fantasy, and it hadn't worked. Yet she couldn't say that she'd disliked the woman. There'd been something about her candid admission regarding the broken engagement that had been oddly touching.

Carlotta's description of Rowan's father had explained in part why her mother had sacrificed everything, including herself, to be with him, but the rest of what she'd been told didn't fit in.

'So you've been getting to know Carlotta,' Rowan's voice said from behind her, and she swung round in surprise.

'Er...yes.'

'And what did she have to say?'

'That you were cold and unrelenting.'

He gave a wintry smile.

'Did she indeed? Well, being cold is something *she* could never be accused of. I must have been out of my mind, getting engaged to someone like her. Life was pretty bleak at the time and I suppose I thought she might bring some brightness into it.'

Rowan wasn't going to tell Davina that his father had just been diagnosed with terminal cancer when he'd met

Carlotta. Yet he wanted to. Just as he wanted to tell Davina that her mother *had* cared about her, cared so much that she'd got herself killed in her desperation to go back for her daughter.

'Can I take you out for a meal somewhere tonight?' he asked. 'Or are you still determined not to hear me out? You're going to be away from the practice for two weeks and I'd told myself it could wait until you came back, but I don't think I should. I admit that I *did* come here for a purpose, as well as to take over the practice. I made a promise and I haven't yet kept it.'

Davina was weakening, longing to know what he had to tell her after all the years of nothing, but there was the attraction between them. *She* was at a disadvantage. Last night she'd told him she was falling in love with him, and at lunchtime in his apartment she'd melted in his arms like butter in the sun. So how could she listen to what he had to say with an unbiased mind?

If he'd come to plead the cause of the runaways, she didn't want to know. What was it that Carlotta had said? His father was handsome and charming and that Rowan was like him. It would be shaming if she fell in love with the son after her mother's affair with the father.

'I'm sorry,' she said, swallowing hard, 'but no. I'm taking the time off to get away from you. I want some space to come to terms with who you are. Since last night I've felt you are playing some sort of game of your own. And as for what happened this morning...'

'You mean when we gave in to the attraction between us?'

'Yes, that. Don't you see that we are the last two people to be sharing those sort of feelings? It's almost obscene.'

'Now you're being ridiculous,' he said flatly. 'I might be called Westlake but I haven't got something catching.'

'Oh, yes, you have!' she cried. 'And if you've had your lunch, I haven't had mine. I'll see you back at the practice.' Leaving him to gaze bleakly after her, she went to the village baker's for a sandwich.

As she was passing her money over the counter to Magda Morris, whose family had owned the business for as long as she could remember, there was a screech of brakes outside the shop followed by screams. When Davina went rushing to the door her blood ran cold. Rowan was lying motionless on the pavement with the wheels of a red sports car almost on top of him.

When she flung herself out of the shop Clive Holden was in front of her, hurrying to the scene of the accident. She threw him her car keys, crying as she ran past, 'Get my bag out of the car, Clive, and then phone for an ambulance.'

Rowan was lying very still with his leg twisted underneath him and she knew immediately that it was broken from the angle of it. That was bad enough, but her main concern was to check if he was breathing.

As she dropped on to her knees beside him she saw that his chest was rising and falling and she sent up a silent prayer of thanks. Next she prised open his mouth to make sure that his tongue hadn't gone back and blocked the airway. Having satisfied herself that was not the case, she unbuttoned his shirt at the neck and felt his pulse.

Her hands were moving fast but she felt as if her mind was paralysed. The doctor in her was coping. The woman in love was in the grip of dread. There were people around but all she was conscious of was Rowan lying so still beside her.

'What happened, for goodness' sake?' she heard some-one ask.

A tremulous female voice said, 'The doctor jumped in front of me when he saw the car mounting the pavement. He saved my life.'

'The ambulance is on its way, Davina,' Clive's voice said from somewhere above her head, and she nodded sombrely, her eyes riveted on Rowan's ashen face.

'Where's the driver of the car?' someone was asking.

'Done a runner,' the landlord of the pub commented. 'He'd been drinking steadily since we opened, and when I refused to serve him any more he stormed off and drove away like a maniac.'

At that moment Rowan groaned and slowly opened his eyes.

'Don't move,' Davina said thickly as relief brought tears with it. 'Your leg is broken from the looks of it. The ambulance is on its way.'

He managed a grimace of a smile.

'Now you see what lengths I'll go to, Davina, to keep you near me,' he mumbled. 'I hope you haven't booked in anywhere for the next two weeks, as you're going to have to run the practice until I'm back on my feet. Will you mind?'

She shook her head. Of course she wouldn't mind. She was so grateful to see him breathing, speaking, observing her rationally with the familiar dark gaze that for once had lost its sparkle.

'No, of course I won't mind,' she said anxiously. 'For-get the practice, Rowan. There are enough of us to keep it ticking over. Lucy is here. I'll tell her to cancel this afternoon's appointments as I'm coming with you to the hospital. I can't believe this has happened. You could have been killed.'

'So could the lady who was just in front of me on the pavement.'

'That was Elaine Boulton, the grandma who's come to live at her son's farm due to a marriage break-up. She's in a state of shock. Lucy's with her.'

He was closing his eyes again and she said anxiously, 'Is it the pain? I can give you an injection.'

'No. I can manage. What about the driver of the car? Is he hurt?'

'We don't know. He panicked and ran off. The land-lord says he'd been drinking all morning and stormed off in a paddy when he wouldn't serve him any more, but he isn't going to get far. They'll get him from the number plate.'

In the ambulance she held his hand and he lay there silently with eyes closed. The paramedics had handled the injured leg with extreme care so as not to damage it further, and as Davina looked down at him she said, 'Do you want me to let your father know?'

'Not unless you have a direct line to the afterlife, Davina.'

'He's dead?'

'Yes. I came to the valley to fulfil his last request.'

Her eyes were wide with shock, but Rowan was in no fit state for questions. He was in a lot of pain, probably facing an operation on his leg, and at that moment he was all that mattered. The rest of it was in the past and she could live with that just as long as Rowan was going to be all right.

Every time she was near him he turned her life upside down but this time it wasn't his fault, and she knew with a deep certainty that whatever disruptions he was causing it was better than never having known him.

CHAPTER FIVE

THEY'D taken Rowan down to Theatre to operate on his leg and Davina was waiting anxiously for him to come back. X-rays had shown a fracture of the shaft of the femur, or thigh bone, and because the bone ends had been displaced in the accident, surgery was necessary.

An orthopaedic consultant had been to see him and explained what Rowan had already worked out for himself, that the affected bone ends would have to be re-aligned with the help of a long metal pin.

A neurologist had also been called to Accident and Emergency to examine a large swelling at the side of his head from when he'd hit the ground at the point of impact.

Davina had been dreading it would turn out to be hae-morrhaging inside the skull in the form of a haematoma, but to her relief X-rays had shown the skull to be clear and the swelling to be normal bruising of tissue.

She'd half expected that would be the result of the X-ray as when she'd felt the swelling in the ambulance it hadn't been soft and squelchy, as with a haematoma.

But there was still the operation to be got through and as they'd wheeled him down to Theatre he'd said, 'Go home, Davina. I'll be all right. I'm not your responsibility.'

'Who says you're not? I'm your doctor, aren't I?'

'Yes, but if it hadn't been for the accident you'd be on holiday now.'

'So what? Do you honestly think I'm going to leave

you here without anyone by your side? Go and get your-self put together again and I'll be here when you come back,' she'd told him, hoping he wouldn't see through her calm exterior to the real feelings beneath.

His face had been grave beneath its pallor.

'I don't deserve you.'

'No, you don't. It must be your lucky day,' she said flippantly, and as the porter had pointed the trolley in the direction of the operating theatre she'd kissed his swollen cheek.

And now it was a case of waiting and offering up silent thanks because it had turned out to be no worse. What she would have done if he'd been killed was something she daren't think about. She loved the man...and how much simpler it would be if she didn't.

When her mobile phone rang Grace's voice came over the line and it was high-pitched with incredulity.

'How is Dr Westlake?' she asked. 'I'd heard there'd been an accident in the village but had no idea that he was involved until they phoned through from the surgery to tell me where you'd gone.'

'He's in Theatre now,' Davina told her, 'being op-erated on for a fractured femur. Rowan saved Elaine Boulton's life and nearly lost his own.'

'And you are devastated?' Grace asked carefully.

'I know I'm a fool. But, yes, I am.'

'It would seem that you are fated to be embroiled with him,' her aunt said. 'I still can't get over the fact that Owen Westlake's son would have the nerve to set up practice here. Have you given any more thought to it?'

'I've thought of nothing else,' she said bleakly. 'I'd booked a fortnight's holiday starting tonight to give me some time to think, but that's gone by the board. I will be needed to run the practice until Rowan is back on his feet again.'

'And have you changed your mind about listening to what he has to say regarding your mother.'

'No. But an ex-fiancée of his turned up today, and from what I discovered from her my mother wasn't around when she visited Rowan's father's home some time ago. What that tells us I don't know. His father was ill at the time and has since died.'

'So where is your mother?'

'I don't know, Aunt Grace. If he hadn't come here I wouldn't be wondering, would I? I just can't believe it. I was content as I was, but now I feel as if the clock is being turned back and I don't want it to be.'

'I wish I could have spared you this,' Grace said. 'In any other circumstances I would have been happy to see you with a man like Rowan Westlake, but every time you look at him you'll be remembering what happened long ago and it's not fair. We've been happy over the years, haven't we? Even your father had achieved some sort of disgruntled contentment and then this has to happen. Shall *I* talk to Dr Westlake when he's recovered from his injuries?'

'No.' Davina said immediately. 'Much as I don't want to drag up the past, I'll talk to him. But at the moment there are more important things to be concerned about than the sins of long ago. There's Rowan himself, his injuries…and the practice. There won't be much time left in my life for anything but coping with the sick and suffering on my own. And let's face it, Aunt Grace, there can't be anything any worse than what I know already about his father and my mother, so it will keep.'

At that moment a nurse appeared to announce that the operation was over and Rowan was in the recovery ward so, telling Grace she would be in touch as soon as she had any news, Davina rang off.

'I want to go to him,' she said, and the nurse eyed her dubiously.

'Are you family?'

Davina shook her head.

'No. I'm Dr Richards. I work with Dr Westlake at the Pennine Practice. He's from down south and I don't think he has any close relatives.'

The nurse smiled.

'Go ahead, then, but, please, don't stay too long.'

'I won't,' she promised. 'I just want him to know I'm there for him when he opens his eyes. Rowan nearly got himself killed earlier today saving someone else from what could have been serious injury or even death. So I can't bear to let him out of my sight.'

'So there's more to it than just working together?' the nurse asked with smiling curiosity.

'Maybe,' she said soberly.

There was a lot more to it. More than the woman in the neat blue uniform could possibly imagine, but as Davina sped down the corridor to find him, at that moment his well-being was all that mattered.

Davina,' Rowan murmured when he opened his eyes. 'You still here? What about our patients?'

'They all know what's happened and that I will be catching up with their appointments tomorrow,' she said gently. 'And in any case, you're a patient, too.'

He groaned.

'An impatient patient, I'm afraid. What a mess! I can't leave you with all the workload.'

'You have no choice.' Her voice broke. 'That maniac could have killed you.'

'Yes, but he didn't so we won't go down that road again. I need to know how long they're going to keep me here. I'm aware that I'm going to have to endure the ghastly ordeal of lying here with my leg in traction until it heals.'

She sighed. 'Rowan, you've only just come round from the anaesthetic and I'm going to be in big trouble if the staff see you getting all steamed up. I've already been told not to stay too long, so I'm going. The practice will be fine. I know that all the staff will rally round to help me so relax and for once let someone else take over.'

'I'd like to know what my nuisance rating is at this moment,' he fretted.

'Nil, with regards to the job. Maximum regarding the other business.'

'Ah, yes, that. Maybe one day we'll get the chance to talk. I have a feeling that my already low place in your esteem will drop to zero when we do.'

She put a gentle finger over his lips.

'Shush. You're supposed to rest after the op. Bye for now, Rowan. I'll see you tomorrow between surgeries.' And off she went, just as a hovering nurse started to move in on them.

The sister was seated at a desk in a small office near the ward door and Davina asked, 'Would you know how long Dr Westlake is likely to be hospitalised, Sister?'

'I couldn't say at the moment,' she replied. 'It will depend on how successful the operation has been and his condition generally, as there is the swelling to the head and various other cuts and bruises. The fracture to the shaft of the femur will have to heal and there is always quite a lot of blood loss from the bone in such cases. The orthopaedic surgeon will be round to see him in the morning and will almost certainly order that he be put on traction.' She smiled, 'I hope he isn't fretting already.'

'Something like that.'

'It's usually the case. Those with busy lifestyles are often the worst patients. But our nursing staff will charm him out of the doldrums.'

Which is more than I'm likely to do, Davina thought dismally. All he can think about is the practice.

The sister's glance was on the slender blonde with the worried blue eyes who, it seemed, was also a doctor.

'I'm sure that seeing you must have cheered him up,' she said. 'Are you his partner?'

Davina felt her colour rise. What was she referring to, the practice or…?

'I'm a trainee GP in the village practice that Rowan…Dr Westlake has recently taken over.'

'Ah. I see. Well, don't concern yourself too much. We'll look after him while you hold the fort.'

Lucky nurses, Davina thought wryly as she waited for a taxi to take her home in the absence of her car.

'How did the operation go?' Grace wanted to know the moment Davina set foot in the house.

'All right, I think,' Davina told her, 'but the healing process will not be as quick as Rowan would like. There will be traction, frequent X-rays, followed by lots of physiotherapy.

'I know you'll think I'm crazy, but I've been wondering if we could have him here once he's back on his feet. The upstairs apartment could create a problem until he's completely mobile. For one thing the stairs are very steep in that old building. I thought we could bring a bed down into the morning room and make it into a sort of bedsit.'

Grace was frowning. 'You've changed your tune since last night, Davina,' she said slowly.

'Yes. I know. But he hadn't risked life and limb for the sake of someone else at that time. I feel it's the least we can do.'

'If Rowan Westlake comes into this house, your father will come back to haunt us. His hatred of that family was always a robust emotion.'

'My dad has gone, Aunt Grace,' she said soberly. 'He ruled the roost while he was here but that doesn't apply any longer. And anyway, it might not come to that. Rowan may not need to come here. From what I've seen of him his recovery will probably be twice as fast as anyone else's.'

She hadn't slept much the night before and Davina didn't sleep much that night either. She kept hearing the screech of brakes and remembering Rowan lying so still on the pavement.

In that moment all her annoyance and distrust of him had vanished. What did anything matter as long as he wasn't dead? she'd thought, and the fates had been kind. He was injured, yes, and quite seriously, but he was alive and likely to remain so.

She wished she hadn't been in such a hurry to suggest that they have him at Heatherlea to convalesce. Grace's lack of enthusiasm was understandable. Her aunt probably thought she was out of her mind, getting involved with him after the previous day's revelations, but the accident had made her realise how much he meant to her.

Yet there was nothing in his manner to say that he felt the same as she did. He was attracted to her. That was clear enough, but she doubted whether his feelings went any deeper than that. All he could think of at the hospital was the practice.

Well, she thought as the clock struck four, she would look after it for him. Keep the place running at its full efficiency, no matter what the cost to herself, if that was what he needed for his peace of mind.

She threw back the bed covers. In silk pyjamas and barefooted she went padding across the yard to Jasper's stable. Surprised to see her at that hour, the horse got to his feet and when she reached out for him he nuzzled against her.

'What am I going to do, Jasper?' she asked him. 'I'm in love with the enemy.'

When Davina phoned the hospital later that morning she was told that Dr Westlake was comfortable. He'd had a good night and was now in traction. The report was re-assuring up to a point but given in typical hospital jargon, and she would dearly have liked to have visited him before morning surgery to see for herself.

But for one thing, she knew she wouldn't be welcome on the ward at such an early hour as he wasn't classed as critical, and for another, having been left in charge of the practice, Rowan would be expecting her to be doing just that, looking after their patients, instead of hovering over his bed.

As those same patients came and went, the questions and comments they had for her were similar from old and young alike. How is the doctor? How serious is it? When will he be back? We were sorry to hear about the accident. It was a brave thing he did.

After patiently providing the answers, Davina decided that a daily bulletin should be put up in the surgery for all the kind enquirers.

She was touched by their concern. Even old Adam Lightfoot, who'd lived in the valley all his eighty-nine years and thought that anyone not born and bred upon its soil was from another planet, asked about him while she was examining him for a chest infection.

'That was a good thing he did for young Boulton's mother,' he grunted. 'I'll bet she's wishing she'd never come back to these parts. But, then, she had no choice.' With a sly look out of the corner of his eye he added, 'Somebody has to look after children who've been deserted by their mothers. I might have set my cap at your Aunt Grace if she hadn't been...'

'Lumbered with me?' Davina asked, amazed at his cheek. She could just see Grace fancying the old reprobate. But when he'd gone she allowed herself a moment of amused satisfaction. Rowan had passed the test. He was no longer the stranger in the camp. Because of yesterday, he was one of them.

As the morning progressed, with its mixture of the serious and the not so serious ailments, Davina was assessing the workload. It was going to be heavy with twice the number of patients to see and house calls to make, but she wasn't daunted.

Lucy must have been having the same thoughts because when the early surgery was over she suggested that for the present Davina pass on to her any patients whose problems were minor. When Megan came in, she had similar thoughts. They were great, she thought. Rowan would be foolish to replace any of them.

She intended to visit him before afternoon surgery once she'd done the home visits. It wouldn't leave her much time but she could go to the hospital again in the evening if she wished.

*   *   *

When Davina had left the previous night Rowan had been too drowsy for any really coherent thought, but with the morning his agile mind was working again in spite of the aches and pains from the accident.

She was in his thoughts constantly and each time she came to mind his face was tender. He couldn't remember when anyone had last been so concerned about him. His mother had died when he'd been young. His father had never been there. His grandmother had been the one who'd really loved him, and with her passing he'd been virtually on his own.

There'd been the romance, if it could be called that, with Carlotta, but she'd cared more about herself than anyone else and he'd soon seen through her.

Then he'd met Davina Richards. He'd come to seek her out in her Pennine valley and from the moment of meeting the attraction she had for him had been blurred with the guilt he felt.

He could still remember his stunned amazement when his father had told him weakly that the woman he'd loved and lost had a daughter who had no idea that her mother had died on the very day she'd deserted her.

He couldn't believe that his father could have kept that from her, all those years. But his grandfather had once told him that Michael Richards had threatened to kill them both and would, no doubt, have been even more eager to carry out his threat with regards to his father if he'd found out that the man who'd stolen his wife had been partly responsible for her death.

So the child, who was now a beautiful young doctor, had never known the truth. But for the present he had to consider the practice first and foremost, and Davina's welfare regarding it.

He couldn't leave her to carry the burden alone. She

was clever and capable, dedicated and hardworking, but even with the two of them it was a busy place. Would his predecessor come back for a few weeks to help out? he wondered, and decided that it was something his practice manager could look into.

It was as Davina was about to set off on her house calls that Kate Wells, the middle-aged practice manager, called her to one side.

'Dr Westlake has been on the phone,' she said. 'He wants me to approach Andrew Swinburn with a view to him helping out in the practice while he's out of action.'

'I see,' Davina said flatly, as all her plans of managing the practice on her own faltered. 'And what did Dr Swinburn say?'

'I can't get hold of him at the moment. I'll try again later.'

'I'm going to see Dr Westlake after I've done my calls,' she told Kate. 'I'll tell him that so far you haven't been able to make contact.'

She would also tell him that she would like to have been consulted first. Especially as she'd assured him that she could cope. If she found that she couldn't then she'd be happy for Andrew to be brought in, but Rowan should at least have given her a chance. It was quite clear that he intended ruling the roost from his hospital bed, so she had better be prepared to be met with a list of instructions whenever she went to visit him.

Yes, but he does own the practice, the voice of reason said, and he didn't ask to be in his present predicament. But it didn't stop her from feeling demoted and deflated.

Her first call of the day was to one of his patients, the wife of the gamekeeper who lived in the lodge at the bottom of the drive of the local manorhouse.

Amy Masters had been diagnosed with ME, myalgic encephalomyelitis, some time ago. Having once been one of the most active women in the valley, the forty-five-year-old was now prone to long bouts of complete exhaustion that left her unable to care for herself or her family.

Her home-made cakes and preserves had always been the highlight at garden parties and church fêtes, but now it sometimes took her all her time just to make a cup of tea. Which left her husband with all the household chores to do as well as his job as gamekeeper to the wealthy landowner in the big house.

A gastric intestinal infection that hadn't cleared up properly had been the cause of the onset of the illness, and from that had come severe muscle fatigue leading to extreme exhaustion, lack of concentration, sleeplessness, nausea and dizziness.

Occasionally when the doctors called on routine visits she would open the door to them like her old self, smiling and energetic, but those times were short-lived and the exhaustion was soon back.

Today a home visit had been asked for. It wasn't routine. With the present workload it was going to be emergencies only, and when the message had come through that Amy had had a fall Davina had decided to make the gamekeeper's cottage her first stop.

She was alone, deathly pale and trembling from head to foot. 'I was coming down the stairs to get a drink,' she said, 'but I was so weak and dizzy my legs just buckled beneath me and I fell when I was halfway down. Jim will go mad. He told me to stay put until he came back. He's up on the moors with his boss.'

'Where does it hurt most?' Davina asked.

'My back. I hit my spine on every step.'

'Can you walk?'

'Just about. I managed to get to the phone.'

'I need to examine you,' Davina told her.

'I haven't the strength to get undressed,' the sick woman said weakly.

'I'll help you. If we just remove your jumper and drop your skirt, I think I can manage.'

There was bruising and discoloration of the back from the waist downwards and swelling around the bottom of the spine and the buttocks, and even though Amy was in no fit state to be taken to A and E, an X-ray was needed to check that none of the vertebrae were damaged.

'I know what you're going to say,' Amy said wearily. 'I have to go for an X-ray.'

Davina flashed her a sympathetic smile. 'I'm afraid so. I'm going to phone for an ambulance, and if your husband has a mobile phone with him I'll let him know what's happening.'

At that moment he came striding up the garden path and Davina thought thankfully that he was just in time to accompany his wife in the ambulance.

As she drove to the next call her thoughts were with the woman she'd just left. ME was a strange and complex illness, not easily diagnosed and often not sympathised with by those who didn't understand it.

It was often thought to be a state of mind rather than a physical illness and sufferers and their families were frequently in a state of complete bewilderment as the malady progressed. There was no definite cure, fast or slow. Amy had been in her present state for four years and there were no signs of the illness having run its course.

It was half past two when Davina arrived at the hospital to visit Rowan, and now that she had time to think about her own affairs she acknowledged that the hurt she'd felt earlier in the day was still there.

There was nothing wrong in asking Andrew Swinburn to help out at the practice, but at least Rowan could have waited until she'd had a chance to show him whether she could cope, and if he hadn't wanted to do that he should have consulted her before he asked for the elderly GP's assistance.

He might be ten years older than her and have a lot more experience than she did, but she was no dumbo and if he wasn't hospitalised she would be telling him so.

As she stopped off at the snack bar in the reception area to buy a sandwich, which was going to be her lunch, she saw Carlotta leaving the building and her eyes widened. How had *she* known where he was? Had he phoned her or asked someone to pass on a message? It didn't look much as if he wanted nothing more to do with her from where she was standing.

He was looking miserable and grumpy as she approached his bed and she hoped it wasn't his ex-fiancée's departure that was spreading the gloom. When he saw her coming towards him, a young, businesslike figure in a navy blazer and grey tailored skirt, above long legs in smart low-heeled shoes, his face cleared.

It was Carlotta's arrival, rather than her departure, that had cast a shadow over his day. Twice in two days was too much. Apparently the newspapers had got hold of the story of yesterday's incident and though the hospital was obeying his wishes and keeping the press away from him, it hadn't stopped Carlotta from taking advantage of the piece in the papers on the chance of some publicity for herself. Once she'd found that it wasn't going to be she'd gone.

What a difference between the two women, he thought. One was the giver, the other the taker. Just the sight of Davina was lifting his spirits. By now she would know he was contemplating asking Andrew to help out at the practice, and she would understand that her welfare was just as important to him as that of their patients.

But when he flashed her a smile she didn't respond, though the anxiety in her glance was lessening. Had she seen Carlotta leaving? he wondered. Was she doubting that he'd really put the actress out of his life? Or was it something else that was making his young assistant look so serious?

'How are you this morning?' she asked as she sank down onto the chair beside the bed.

'Like a caged animal,' he said wryly. 'In more ways than one. My mind is working flat out, but the leg and the rest of a rather sore anatomy is static. I'm going to have to learn patience, I'm afraid. But that's enough about me, Davina. How's it going at the practice?'

'Fine so far,' she said, still without the smile he was waiting for. 'Lucy and Megan are attending to the patients with minor problems and I'm dealing with the others. I've just finished the home visits and am going to eat my lunch while I'm here if you don't mind.'

Rowan frowned.

'By all means do so, but I hope it will be the only instance of you not having time to eat. I've asked Kate to get in touch with Andrew Swinburn to see if he'll help out.'

'So I believe,' she said frostily.

'There seems to be a sudden drop in temperature. Any reason?'

'Of course there's a reason,' she snapped. 'First of

all you might have asked my opinion about bringing Andrew in.'

'And?'

'Secondly, it's hardly a show of confidence in me when you're looking for extra help before I've even had the chance to show I can cope. It's a rural practice we're talking about, busy enough in its way but with patients who will understand if the service is a bit slower, especially as the situation has arisen because the new doctor almost got himself killed helping one of them.'

'I see,' he said tightly. 'So the fact that I'm concerned about your welfare just as much or even more than everyone else's is a source of irritation.'

She was hating herself now for bringing the subject up. But knowing Rowan, once he'd tuned in to her annoyance he wouldn't have let it rest until she'd told him the cause of it.

Unbelievably, like someone with a death wish, she was about to make matters worse.

'And was it concern for me that brought you to the valley? Sneaking into my life to steal my peace of mind?'

His dark gaze was cold now. There were no more smiles for her.

'I didn't even know you existed until recently…and I didn't *sneak* anywhere. I bought the practice openly, and the reason I didn't rush into telling you who I am is because I was bringing you great hurt. I felt like the messenger of doom and it wasn't a role I was happy to play.'

'So where *is* my mother? Carlotta never saw her when she visited your father's house, and if he's dead what is she doing now that she's been left on her own?'

'You have some more visitors, Dr Westlake, and you're only allowed two at a time,' a nurse said from behind, and when Davina turned round she saw Elaine Boulton and her son hovering awkwardly in the doorway.

'I want to be on my feet when I answer that question,' he said in a low voice as Davina got up to make way for the others.

It was true. If she were to flee from him in anguish when she heard what he had to say, he had to be able to follow her, comfort her and ask forgiveness for the wrongs his father had done her.

And if that didn't put out the spark that their attraction for each other had ignited, then nothing would. Forcing himself to look cheerful, he prepared to greet the Boultons.

He could imagine how Elaine was feeling, seeing him battered and bruised and all strung up, but it wasn't her fault, or his. He wondered if the driver of the car had been found. Hopefully he might have learned his lesson, but it wasn't always the case. Not when the taste for alcohol was stronger than the dictates of common sense.

CHAPTER SIX

WHEN Davina arrived back at the practice Kate said, 'I've managed to get hold of Andrew Swinburn's house-keeper. He's away for the next two weeks.'

'I see,' Davina said slowly.

So unless Rowan brought in someone new when he heard that, it was going to be how she wanted it. On her own until the retired GP came back from wherever he'd gone.

'I'm going to phone Dr Westlake for further instructions,' Kate said. 'Have you any comments you wish me to pass on?'

Davina shook her head.

'No. I've already said what I have to say to him. We are not in agreement about staffing the practice while he's out of action. I shall call in to see him again this evening and no doubt he'll want to discuss it then. I want to try coping on my own and will admit it if I can't, but he didn't seem too confident of my ability to do so.'

With that she left Kate to make the phone call to Rowan and went to give Reception a bulletin to put up on his progress.

'So what's the verdict?' the staff wanted to know. 'How *is* Dr Westlake?'

Davina gave a wry smile. 'Bossy and difficult, but progressing satisfactorily under the circumstances.'

'I take it that the first part of that was for our ears only,' Lucy said laughingly, and there were smiles all round. They'd all had time to size him up and knew that the enforced inactivity would not be suiting the new GP.

It was half past six when Davina drew up outside Heatherlea and Grace was out in the porch to greet her the moment she heard the sound of the car engine.

'How is the patient and what sort of a day have you had?' she asked as her niece swung long legs out of the car and stretched herself wearily.

Davina smiled. 'Rowan seems to be progressing all right, but is frustrated and edgy.'

'Which is not surprising under the circumstances,' Grace remarked.

Davina nodded. 'And as to the kind of day I've had, it's been a mixture of a lot of things. At this moment I'm experiencing a sort of tired satisfaction. I've coped without him and there have been no major hiccups. Rowan has asked Kate to bring Andrew in to assist me without asking my opinion. It caused us to have a few sharp words as I saw it as lack of confidence in me.'

Grace was observing her thoughtfully with lips pursed and head to one side. 'So you don't think it was concern for you that prompted the suggestion.'

'It might have been, but he should still have asked me first.'

'It is *his* practice.'

'Yes. I know it is, but I can feel in my bones that the Westlake family are going to continue being a thorn in our side.'

'I thought you were attracted to him.'

She sighed. 'Yes, I am. That's the trouble. I would give anything for him to be called Smith or Jones.'

'Come and have your meal,' Grace said, patting her

niece gently on the top of her golden bob, 'and then you must have a nice restful evening.'

'I can't,' Davina said wryly. 'I need to see Rowan again.'

'Need as in practice matters? Concern over his welfare? Or need as in longing to be with him?'

'A bit of all three, but mostly the last.'

'That's what I was afraid of,' Grace said as she went into the kitchen to dish up. 'On the face of it Rowan Westlake is everything I could want for you in a man, but your life has already been marred by the father. I wouldn't like the son to follow in his footsteps.'

'Don't you think I haven't considered that?' she said wearily. 'Yet it seems to make no difference. All I know is that I need to be where Rowan is…and don't forget, I'm not my mother. I'm a tougher creature than she was…from a different generation.'

'Love can be a hurtful thing no matter what generation you're from,' Grace warned. 'The ups and downs of a romantic affair don't change with age. Promise me you'll be sensible in your dealings with this man. Don't let him break your heart.'

'I promise,' Davina said, and meant it until the moment she arrived at the side of Rowan's bed and looked down at him, sleeping with his face screwed up in a frown and one arm hanging limply over the side.

He looked oddly defenceless lying there. Taking advantage of his unawareness of her presence, she stood drinking in the moment. Her hand went out to touch his cheek, but she drew back as he spoke in his sleep.

'Dead,' he mumbled. 'Isabel's dead.'

As she stood transfixed at his side he groaned and moved his head restlessly on the pillow. Then, as if sensing her presence, he opened his eyes and after a moment's surprised silence he said, 'Davina! You're back. I must have fallen asleep.'

She was observing him unsmilingly. 'Yes, you had. And like lots of folk with a troubled mind you were talking in your sleep.'

The dark eyes looking up at her were suddenly wary, but he made his voice sound casual as he asked, 'And what was I saying?'

'You said that my mother is dead,' she told him in a voice that was ragged with shock.

He raised a hand to his head and raked through his hair distractedly.

'Oh, no! I didn't, did I? That was the message I brought. What I came to tell you. So far I'd never found the right moment and now I go and blurt it out in my sleep. What an idiot!'

Davina had sunk down onto the chair beside the bed, her face white, her legs shaking.

'How recent was it?' she asked. 'Before or after your father?'

Rowan reached out and took her hand and, taking a deep breath, he passed on the hurt that he had been pledged to bring.

'She died when they crashed the car on the very day they left here together all those years ago,' he said gently. 'She wanted my father to go back for you but he wouldn't. Not without reason as he saw it, as your father had threatened to shoot the pair of them. But your frantic mother saw it from a very different viewpoint and when he refused she grabbed the steering-wheel to try to turn the car round. They hit a tree and she was killed instantly.

'My father wanted you to know that she really did love you. That it was a mother's deep love and devotion that made her react so irrationally. It was never her intention

to leave you. The thing uppermost in her mind was going
back to get you. I'm so sorry that it has taken all this
time for you to learn the truth. My father did you another
great wrong there. But now you know that she has not
been keeping away from you all these years. She would
never have done that. You need to know that only death
stopped her from showing you how much she loved you.
It was my father's dying wish that you should know that.'

I'm going to be sick, Davina thought as the walls of
the ward tilted in on her. How could Owen Westlake
have done that to her? In her most private thoughts over
the years she'd dreamed that one day she might see her
mother again, when all the time there hadn't been the
faintest chance of that ever happening. How could he
have been so cruel?

Her father had gone to his grave never knowing her
mother was dead, which was awful, too, but knowing the
kind of man he'd been he probably wouldn't have cared
anyway.

Davina got to her feet like someone old and infirm,
holding onto the arms of the chair for support.

Rowan said tightly, 'Don't go, Davina. This was the
last thing I wanted to happen. You've had an awful
shock. You can see why I didn't want to tell you, can't
you? But now that you know I'll want to be there for
you while you're coming to terms with it.'

'And do you think *I* want that?' she said flatly. 'After
what your family has done to me?'

Before he could reply she began to walk away from
him with dragging steps, and as he lay there helpless all
Rowan's worst fears were being realised.

He cursed the day that his father had told him Isabel
had a daughter. Wrapped up in his own grief, almost to
the point of being a recluse, Owen had denied Davina

the truth about her mother, and she'd grown up believing that her mother didn't love her. And now, at a time when it could have been the start of something wonderful for them both, he'd had to ruin it because of a promise made to a dying man.

His gaze went to his leg, strung up on high, and if he could have got his hands on the drunken motorist he would have throttled him. But it was no use ranting and railing about what the fates were handing out. The essential thing was to do what he could for Davina, and a phone call to Grace would have to be his next move.

'Oh, no!' she said when she'd heard what he had to say. 'That is dreadful. The poor girl. Where is Davina now?'

'On her way home, I hope,' he said sombrely. 'I can imagine what you're thinking of me at this moment, but could you, please, ring me back when she gets in so that I know she's arrived safely?'

'Yes. I'll do that,' she promised coldly, and left him to his miserable thoughts.

When Davina went out into the hospital grounds she leant against the wall with head bent. The nausea was passing but her skin felt cold and clammy and the doctor in her was telling her to go and find a cup of hot sweet tea.

The same refreshment kiosk as where she'd bought her lunch earlier in the day was still open and seating herself at a small table she began to sip the steaming brew.

So it's over, she thought. End of story. The runaway lovers had fared no better, even worse, than the rest of them. There had been punishment all round, and to cap it all it had taken the man she'd fallen in love with to deliver the final blow.

She was glad that he wasn't able to follow her, she

told herself. Glad! With Rowan in the hospital it wouldn't
be difficult to avoid him, and that was what she wanted.
Time to adjust. Time to take stock. Time to forget him.
Though how she was going to do that once he was back
in charge of the practice she didn't know. Maybe it was
time to move on, but not yet. She couldn't leave him in
the lurch in his present state.

She could see Grace watching for her anxiously as she
pulled up in front of the house and the calm she'd found
during those moments in the café and on the way home
was shattered when her aunt held out her arms.

'Can you believe it, Aunt Grace?' she sobbed. 'She's
been dead all those years and we didn't know. I hate that
family.'

'Shush,' Grace soothed. 'I know how you're hurting
but, Davina, you have to remember that Rowan knew
nothing about you. He was left to do the dirty work and
it can't have been easy. At least you know now how
much Isabel loved you.'

'I know. And I can't tell you how much that means to
me, but he's a Westlake,' she said stubbornly, 'and
what's more, I had to hear it from him while he was
asleep!'

'I'll bet he's not too happy about that,' her aunt remarked with a grim smile. 'The next time you go to see
him you both need to have a long talk. It's all out in the
open now. Nothing more to hide. The way forward is
open to both of you. He's done what he was asked to do
and you know the truth at last.'

'I don't want to see him until I have to. There are
plenty of other folk who can visit him.'

'Such as?'

'The staff from the practice. His actress friend. She
was just leaving as I got there.'

'They're not family, though.'

'Neither am I.'

'You might have been if things had worked out differently. Stepbrother…and -sister.'

'Yes, well, we're not, and will you stop pleading his cause, Aunt Grace? It's almost as if you sympathise with him.'

'I do in a way, but I'm also very aware that he's brought you sorrow and I do so wish he hadn't, for both your sakes. But he's also brought you relief.'

Over the next few days Rowan phoned frequently but Davina refused to talk about anything other than practice matters. She felt guilty at the thought of him lying helpless and frustrated when he was so desperate to put things right between them, but her feelings regarding his revelations about her mother's death hadn't changed.

'His father was responsible for what happened to my mother,' she protested when Grace suggested that she should try to forgive and forget and go to see him. 'If he hadn't persuaded her to go away with him, it would never have happened.'

'You're not being fair there,' her aunt said. 'Your mother might never have left if your father hadn't been so violent towards them. He would have carried out his threats if they hadn't fled…and Isabel *was* the one who sent the car out of control, remember.'

'It doesn't alter the fact that Rowan came here without telling me who he was, and there was I falling all over him, totally at a disadvantage. He knew who I was, but I was completely in the dark. Why couldn't I fall in love with someone less complicated? Like Jack Morrison or even pushy Clive.'

Grace smiled. 'That's soon answered. Put those two beside Rowan Westlake and they are nothing.'

The discussion had ended there because there was nowhere else for it to go, and as the days went by Davina had to rely on reports of Rowan's progress from those on the staff who'd popped in to see him…and from Grace.

'I've been to see Rowan today,' she said one night when Davina arrived home after a long hard day at the practice.

'Really? And did he have any more dark secrets from the past that he's omitted to mention?' she asked coolly as her heartbeat quickened.

Grace shook her head. 'No. He's hoping that it's the end of it.'

'Is he? Thinks it's as easy as that, does he?'

'Rowan was also virtually cut off from his parent. After he lost your mother Owen went working abroad, leaving his son in the care of his grandparents.'

'Maybe. But at least he knew where his father was. He was living and breathing…'

'So you're not going to go and see him.'

Davina sighed. 'I will have to eventually, won't I? We work together. But that is going to change once Rowan is on his feet.'

'So you're not going to let him down while he's incapacitated?'

'No. *I'm* not going to let *him* down. If I did that I'd be letting the folks of the valley down, too. So I shall stay put until he comes back.'

'And what then?'

'Something will turn up. I'm too busy at the moment to give it too much thought.'

It was true. Every moment of the day was spoken for.

It was a fortnight since the accident and she was realising that Rowan had been right when he'd suggested they should bring Andrew in to help. She was exhausted, but no way was she going to admit it. Not to him anyway.

But when the elderly GP appeared one morning, looking fit and tanned after two weeks in Spain, she found relief sweeping over her.

'So what's this I hear about Dr Westlake?' he asked as he perched on the corner of her desk. 'He's the local hero I believe. And you, my dear girl, look extremely tired. Lizzie, my housekeeper, tells me you could do with some help.'

'Yes, please,' she said with a smile for the man she'd known all her life. 'I've been managing, but only just. Rowan wanted to bring in extra help for me right from the beginning but I refused and now I'm beginning to feel the strain.'

'Not surprising. I'd had years of experience but I still found it exhausting, running this place on my own. Give me a few moments to get settled in his consulting room and then start directing the sick and suffering in my direction.'

She was serious now. 'Before you go, can I ask you something?'

He paused in the doorway. 'Fire away.'

'When Rowan Westlake took over the practice, did you know he was the son of the man that my mother went away with?'

Bushy grey brows rose in surprise.

'No. I didn't. Yet maybe I should have. Thinking back, the name is familiar. But the last thing I would have expected was for anyone from that family to come to live in these parts. I would have warned you if I'd known. So what's happened?'

'I didn't know who he was to begin with, but Aunt Grace recognised the name and then it all came out. My mother was killed in a car crash on the very day they left here, and I've only just found out.'

'That's bad, Davina. But maybe now is the time for you to decide that what happened long ago is a closed book. In a strange sort of way Westlake might have done you a favour.'

'I'm afraid that I can't see it like that,' she said dismally. 'I feel as if I don't want anything more to do with him.'

But it wasn't that easy. Inside she was weakening. When Rowan came on the phone to talk about practice matters she ached to see him, to touch him, to forgive him, but felt it would be a betrayal of her mother if she did...so all they did was discuss health care. He'd given up on what there had been between them, and where she should have been relieved now she was wishing he hadn't.

There was just one comforting thought to be had from the whole sorry business, she kept telling herself, and it was that her mother hadn't really deserted her. She'd got herself killed because she couldn't bear to leave her behind, and it was something to hold onto in the dark hours of the night when she longed to go to Rowan and beg him to hold her close.

But there was coldness in his voice now. The pleading was over, just like the chemistry that had sprung up between them. And she didn't know whether to be glad or sorry.

With the arrival of Andrew at the practice she was feeling less tense and not as tired as the days went by, which gave her more time to think. She'd phoned Rowan to tell him that Andrew was back from holiday and al-

ready in harness and had expected him to say 'I told you
so', but he'd merely commented in the cold clipped voice
that was becoming familiar, 'Good. Ask him to call in
and see me so that we can discuss salary arrangements
and hours.'

There'd been no enquiries as to whether she was glad
of the extra help or otherwise, and she was determined
that *she* wasn't going to bring the subject up, so the
phone call had been like the others, brief and unsatisfac-
tory.

When he'd replaced the receiver Rowan had lain back
against the pillows with relief washing over him. Davina
was getting some help at last and from the best possible
source, the man who'd spent most of his working life
looking after the health of the valley folk.

She wasn't going to admit she was happy about it, of
course. That would mean acknowledging he'd done
something right for once, and that would never do.

He was resigned now to not seeing her during the long
miserable days, but his time would come. He wouldn't
be strung up for ever and once he got back to the practice
they were going to talk about themselves whether she
liked it or not.

Grace had been to see him a couple of times and he
felt that she understood more than her niece the predicament that his father had placed him in. But her loyalties
were with Davina and he couldn't blame her for that.
They'd both been innocent victims...if Davina would
only see it that way.

It was midsummer, a warm mellow night, and with new-
found time on her hands Davina was restless and on edge.
Watching her, Grace knew why, but was loath to make
any comment.

Any move towards a reconciliation with Rowan had to come from Davina herself, she thought. If she loved him enough, one day she would accept him for who he was with no strings attached.

'Shall we have a walk down to the pub?' she suggested as Davina wandered from room to room.

Her thoughts far away beside a hospital bed, Davina eyed her blankly for a moment and then said, 'Er… yes…if you like. I suppose it's better than sitting around doing nothing. I've been so busy of late I'm finding it hard to unwind.'

When they reached the main street of the village it was as if the warm night had brought everyone outside. A group of teenagers were making eyes at each other on the seats by the war memorial and the beer garden at the back of the pub was full.

Davina's mood was lightening with the change of scene, until they came to the baker's shop and she looked across to where she'd seen Rowan lying so ominously still on the pavement.

She'd passed the spot countless times since the accident and had looked away, but tonight her eyes were drawn to it as if some unseen force was controlling them. And suddenly all that mattered was that he was alive.

When she halted in mid-stride Grace said, 'What is it?'

'I'm going back to get the car,' she told her, 'and then I'm going to see Rowan.'

Grace smiled.

'Good thinking. It's gone on long enough.'

Her step was buoyant, her resolve firm, until she reached the ward and saw the empty bed.

'Dr Westlake has been discharged,' a nurse said when

she saw Davina's expression. 'He went home by ambulance an hour ago.'

'I see,' she said slowly. 'Are the staff here aware that he lives in an upstairs apartment above the surgery? Is he going to be able to negotiate the stairs?'

'The paramedics will get him safely up there,' the nurse said. 'And if he does have any difficulty once he's settled it will be a case of staying put while the physiotherapy that he's been having here is continued until the leg is fully mobile.'

Bang goes my idea of having him at Heatherlea, Davina thought. Maybe under the circumstances it was just as well. And wasn't it typical of Rowan that he hadn't told anyone he was being discharged? He was just too independent for words. If he didn't want anything to do with her any more he could have told someone else on the staff that he was coming home. There would be no food in the apartment, no clean sheets on the bed.

'But he lives alone,' she protested.

The nurse smiled. 'Yes, so I believe. Incredible, an attractive man like that. There are one or two here on the nursing staff who would be there if he beckoned. I'm sure that someone will be only too happy to look after his needs.'

'Yes, no doubt they will,' Davina said deflatedly as she turned around. And how was he going to react if it was *she* who stepped into the role of carer? Would he eye her askance after weeks of brief, cold, telephone conversations?

If he did, it wouldn't matter. She was going to the apartment now. She'd neglected him long enough and, if he saw it as a quick about-turn because he was back on the premises and could no longer be avoided, she would have to put up with it.

* * *

When Davina let herself into the practice there was silence up above, and she went to the bottom of the stairs and called Rowan's name.

'Come up, if you must,' he answered, and on that less than cordial invitation she ascended.

He was seated in a chair by the window with crutches at one side of him and a holdall waiting to be unpacked at the other. If it had involved anyone else the scene might have seemed forlorn but not with him. Rowan looked pleased with himself and relaxed, though he wasn't throwing any smiles in her direction when she appeared.

'Why didn't you let me know you were being discharged?' she asked with a fast-beating heart as she went to stand beside him.

'Are you joking?' he hooted. 'You haven't been near me for weeks. If you'd been in touch you would have known.'

'I thought that we *were* in touch. We've spoken on the phone every day.'

'Don't pretend that you don't understand me, Davina,' he said levelly. 'And what are you here for now? Certainly not the big reconciliation scene, I would imagine.'

As she opened her mouth to tell him that *was* why she was there, he went on, 'Because if you are, save your breath. All I ever did wrong was to hesitate in telling you who I was and what I'd come for…and do you know why I did that? It was because once I'd met you I couldn't bear the thought of hurting you and ruining the rapport we had.'

She became angry. 'And that makes it all right, does it? By all means justify yourself and make me look unreasonable. But I'm not here to argue, Rowan.'

She moved towards the kitchen and she bent and opened the fridge door.

'It's just as I thought. You've no food apart from frozen stuff. I'm going to go across to the late night shop and buy the essentials. When I get back I'll put clean sheets on the bed and then, as long as I'm satisfied that you are mobile enough to cope, I shall leave you, as my presence is so unwelcome.

'The nurse I spoke to this evening said that you'll be confined up here until you're able to move freely, which is understandable as the stairs are so steep, but at least you'll have your finger on the pulse more with the practice. I'd suggested to Aunt Grace that you come to stay with us when you were discharged, but you didn't give me the chance to offer—though I must admit that I've had second thoughts since...'

'Since you found me difficult and devious?'

'You had just cause to be difficult. It must have been very frustrating for you, being cooped up like that. But devious is another matter. Trust is vital in any relationship and in ours it seems a rare commodity—but enough of going round in circles. I have to see to stocking your fridge.'

'You've certainly got your "I'm in charge" hat on,' he said with a grim smile. 'Roll on the day when I'm back at the controls.'

There was no reply. Davina was halfway down the stairs, making a list as she went.

What was the matter with him? Rowan thought when she'd gone. He'd been aching for the sight of her and the moment Davina had appeared he'd been snappy and self-righteous.

He couldn't believe she'd considered inviting him to

complete his recovery at Heatherlea, even though she had had second thoughts. He would have loved to have been under the same roof in the house that had always been her home.

In fact, any roof anywhere would do if they were beneath it together. But they weren't making much progress towards that. Instead of treading carefully, he was trampling all over her because she wasn't falling into the mould he wanted her in.

When she came back he was where she'd left him, gazing through the window at the sun setting over the peaks. After depositing the groceries on the kitchen table she went to stand by him, drawn to his side as if by a magnet.

He turned and, reaching out for her, took her hands in his.

Encouraged by the gesture, Davina dropped to her knees beside him and, looking into his eyes, said softly, 'I'm glad you're home for your sake. I know how hard it must have been, lying on your back all day when you needed to be up and moving.'

'It wasn't made any easier by not seeing you,' he told her dryly. 'If I hadn't been burbling in my sleep, it wouldn't have come to that, would it?'

'You would have had to tell me some time.'

'Yes. I know. But I wanted it to be when the moment was right.'

'It would never have been the right time for that sort of news. The pain of it will never go away.'

'So I'm still not forgiven?'

'I don't want to talk about it any more. You're home now and everything will soon be back to normal here. Once you're really fit again I'm contemplating moving to a city health centre. They are more impersonal than a village practice. Difficult relationships aren't as likely to develop.'

His face had tightened. His jaw bone was jutting against the skin.

'So that's what you've catalogued our feelings for each other as…a difficult relationship. Well, I don't see it like that,' he said with sudden savagery. 'I'm not making any excuses for the past, but I am going to make a few strikes for the future. If you're a defeatist, *I'm* not!'

She was still in a kneeling position and when his arms came out to encircle her it was only seconds before his mouth claimed hers. His kiss went on and on until, gasping for breath, she pushed him away.

'Now tell me that you don't love me!' he said softly as she sank limply back on her heels.

'I love *what* you are,' she said weakly as she got slowly to her feet, 'but not *who* you are. You are Owen Westlake's son. If I married you I would be a Westlake and I couldn't face that!'

'So my name puts me beyond the pale?'

He was rising, too, easing himself carefully onto the crutches, and when she stepped forward to help him he said, 'Don't, Davina. You might catch something. Thanks for getting the groceries. You can let yourself out, can't you?'

With the feeling that she'd just been well and truly put in her place, she went.

CHAPTER SEVEN

As THE days went by and Rowan's mobility increased, Davina's decision to leave the practice was faltering. The valley, with the gorse-and heather-covered peaks towering above it, was the place where she wanted to be, with those who were her friends as well as her patients.

She kept telling herself that she would be stifled working in the noise and bustle of the city. There would be no fresh, tangy winds there, or capricious moorland mists that came and went as fast as the clouds scudding across the sky.

Most of all, there would be no dark-eyed doctor eyeing her thoughtfully and keeping his own counsel, as had been the case ever since the night he'd been discharged from hospital.

She knew he hadn't forgotten what she'd said about leaving the practice and that he was waiting to see what she would do. If only he would ask her not to go, she kept thinking, but with each passing day it seemed that he had no intention of doing any such thing.

He'd made it clear that any guilt he'd been carrying around had been absolved now she knew the truth about what had happened to her mother, and that he was prepared to carry on as if they were like any other two people caught up in a strong attraction.

But although she'd found herself in his arms and grasped the moment, there had been no lasting peace between them. Whenever she went up to the apartment to discuss practice matters he was pleasant, polite and extremely businesslike. Every time she tried to break down the barrier between them the words stuck in her throat.

He wasn't like that when the physiotherapist came, she noticed. He was lit up like a beacon as he waited to greet her at the top of the stairs, and once, when Davina needed to speak to him while he was having the treatment, she found Rowan and Alison Symmonds very much at home with each other. Alison had recently opened a private clinic in the village and was similar in appearance to Carlotta.

As Davina went glumly back to her patients, she thought that whatever feelings Rowan might have for herself he was certainly more at ease with the dark voluptuous types.

She'd gone up to see him about an elderly patient who was asking for a smear test. The woman had last had one done five years previously after one or two abnormal results. The practice she'd been registered with at the time had assured her they were not uncommon due to body changes in older women and her last test had shown her to be clear.

But the patient was concerned that it was five years since she'd last had a smear. She was in her midseventies and Davina knew that a woman of that age would not normally be tested again as it was pointless due to the flatness of the cells in that area.

Yet she wasn't prepared to take it upon herself to refuse her request and, as Andrew was out on house calls, she'd gone up to ask Rowan's advice.

He'd read through the patient's notes carefully, giving particular attention to the previous smear test reports, and had said, 'There was nothing serious in her past results. Assure the lady that we see no cause for a further test, just as long as she isn't getting any sinister symptoms.'

'I've asked her that and she isn't,' she'd told him, acutely conscious that the light-hearted laughter and matey chatter had been put on hold with her arrival.

Why couldn't *they* be like that? she thought after she'd told the patient what Rowan had said and she'd gone away reassured. But with every other woman Rowan came into contact with there was no debris to be cleared away. They could start on an even footing. There were no guilt complexes and recriminations to come to terms with.

'And so *are* you going to leave the practice when Rowan is back at the helm?' Grace asked that night.

'I don't know,' Davina said dejectedly. 'I don't want to go. I love it here in the valley, but everything is so mixed up between Rowan and I. Everyone else thinks he's wonderful. The new physio in the village is all over him like a rash. The staff at the practice hang on his every word, and he and Andrew are getting on like a house on fire. Andrew goes round in the evenings to keep Rowan company. All of which leaves me as the odd one out.'

Grace put a comforting arm around her drooping shoulders.

'No one understands how you feel more than I do. You've been through a lot and my heart aches at the thought of you having fallen in love with Rowan, only to have your happiness blighted by the miserable past.'

'But, Davina, that's what it is—the past. Nothing is going to change it, so why don't you accept Rowan for what he is…the innocent son of the man who took your mother from you? The sins of the fathers are often visited on the children, but they shouldn't be.'

'It's too late,' Davina said dejectedly. 'He doesn't want to know. He sees himself as blameless and I'm the un-reasonable one.'

Grace said gently, 'We all say things we don't mean in times of stress. How about offering an olive branch in the form of an invitation to dine with you here at Heatherlea? I could make you both a nice meal for when the late surgery is over and then make myself scarce. When is he due to be back in circulation?'

'Rowan starts back at the surgery next week. He's still a bit stiff-legged but should be able to walk unaided by that time.'

'So leave it until then. Describe it as a meal to celebrate his recovery. It's the kind of invitation any friend would come up with.'

'I'm not even sure if I come into *that* category these days. I'm just the trainee at the practice,' she said wryly, 'but I'll ask him and it will be interesting to see what he says.'

The next day she went up to the apartment after morning surgery. She'd waited until Alison had been and gone and he was alone. The last thing she needed was an audience if he was going to refuse the invitation.

'Davina!' he said when he opened the door to her. 'To what do I owe this pleasure? Patient problems?'

She shook her head. 'No. It's a social call.'

'Really! Then do come in and take a seat. I take it surgery's over.'

She sighed. Was that a reminder where her duties lay? 'Yes. I shall be setting off on the home visits shortly,' she said coolly.

He smiled. 'This time next week I will be doing the same, and it can't come quickly enough.'

'It's about next week that I wanted to talk to you.'

'Yes?'

'I wondered if you'd like to come to Heatherlea for a meal one night to celebrate your recovery.'

'Really!' he said again, and she wished he wouldn't make it sound so surprising that she was there in his apartment and asking him to dine with her. Yet she supposed she couldn't blame him for that, after not visiting him in hospital and continuing to keep her distance since he'd come home.

'That would be very nice, thank you,' he said with measured enthusiasm. 'What night did you have in mind?'

'Whenever it suits you.'

'Thursday, then. Andrew is coming round for a game of chess on Tuesday, and I've promised to take Alison for a drink one evening to say thanks for the magic she's worked on my leg.'

'Yes, she seems very competent,' Davina said with a noticeable lack of enthusiasm.

Rowan didn't comment, just nodded and waited to see if she had anything else to say. When it appeared that she hadn't he broke into the silence to ask, 'And what's happening in *your* life at the moment?'

Davina looked tired, he thought. Her eyes were big in her face, her mouth drooping, and tenderness washed over him. Life hadn't been very kind to her and he was trying not to make it any worse, but at least she had made a gesture. She'd invited him to dine at Heatherlea, so he wasn't entirely a lost cause.

'Not a lot,' she said in answer to his question. 'Just work and sleep.'

'So you're not gallivanting out every night.'

He kept imagining her with some strapping farmer like the Morrison guy, or one of the hunting, shooting, fishing types that he'd seen around the village.

'Not after a day in this place,' she told him dryly. 'Maybe I'll perk up when you are back in the surgery.

When is Andrew going to return to the joys of retirement?'

'I'm not sure. I wanted to discuss it with you first.' He gave a quizzical smile. 'I haven't forgotten your comments when I told Kate to ask him to help us out without consulting you. So what *do* you think?'

'I think it would be a good idea if he stayed on for another week, so that there will be three of us during that time. You've been away from the practice for quite a long period and are bound to find those first few days tiring without the support of the crutches.'

It was on the tip of his tongue to tell her that he'd put up with worse than that in his time, but her concern was something not to be mocked so he said meekly, 'Yes. I think you're right. We'll do that if he's agreeable.'

Davina checked the time. 'I must go.'

'How many calls are there today? You look as if you could do with a rest,' he said, and knew that wasn't going to go down too well.

'I'm all right,' she assured him coolly. 'It's just that I'm not sleeping properly.'

'Why do you think that is?'

'You know why.'

'Do I?'

'Yes. It's because we're at odds with each other.'

'And who is to blame for that?'

'We both are.'

'But I'm more at fault than you?'

'I didn't say that.'

'Come here, Davina,' he said softly, and as she moved slowly towards him he carefully put the crutches to one side and put his arms around her. Holding her gaze, he told her, 'I'm proud of you. Proud of the way you've coped without me. You're a good doctor, Davina. In a few years' time there'll be no touching you for excellence. You're hardworking, kind to the patients and intelligent. I'm lucky to have you here with me. But if you do decide that you can't stand working with me any more, I'll understand. No one loves the bearer of sad tidings. Especially when they are as long overdue as the ones I brought you.'

She could feel Rowan's breath on her face, smell his aftershave, but his nearness wasn't awakening her senses as it had done on other occasions. Tears were spilling down her cheeks and they weren't for the sadness he'd brought with him.

She was weeping for the blight it had put on her love for him, and as he cradled her to him and stroked her hair gently she knew that he thought it was grief for her mother that was making her sob.

'Don't cry, Davina,' he said gently. 'Isabel wouldn't want you to grieve any more. She would want you to get on with your life.'

'I was…until you came along,' she choked, and as his face twisted she knew that he had no answer to that.

'I have to go,' she said, moving away. 'Andrew has already set off on his rounds and if I don't move it will be time for the late surgery before I get back.'

He was observing her sombrely. 'Wait until you've calmed down before driving. Promise me.'

She nodded. 'I promise. I'll make a quick cup of tea before I go.'

'Thanks again for the invitation,' he said as she moved towards the door, and Davina thought that no one would ever guess from the tone of his voice that she'd just been weeping her heart out in his arms.

They were no nearer to putting the past behind them, Rowan thought sombrely when Davina had gone. If she was still so grief stricken after all these weeks, what chance was there for them?

He was the villain of the piece and nothing was going to change that because Davina's hurt went too deep. Was he a fool to go to Heatherlea next week? It was certain to be a constrained affair. He would have to rely on Grace to keep things light. She wasn't as averse to him as Davina. The woman who'd brought Davina up understood his misery, but whether she would approve of him as a husband for her niece was another matter. He'd like to bet that anyone would be looked on with a more favourable eye than him.

But there *was* one thing to be cheerful about. Next week they would be working together again. No longer a prisoner in the apartment, he would be where he liked to be—in the thick of things. And if the only conversations they had were about the ailments of the valley folk, at least it would be better than not communicating at all.

On the Monday morning there was a new lightness in her step as Davina arrived at the practice. Like Rowan, she had decided that being together during daylight hours in the surgery was better than nothing…and there was Friday night to look forward to, though how that would work out she wasn't sure, but at least he'd accepted the invitation.

She'd given Grace a loving squeeze when she'd passed on the news that he was coming and had told her, 'It was a great idea of yours to ask him round. I only hope Rowan won't think it's a set-up when he finds you missing.'

Her aunt had laughed. 'Rowan will probably be delighted to have you to himself, as I'm sure there isn't much chance of that at the practice.'

'There is no chance at all,' she'd said with a wry smile, 'and don't be too sure he'll want me to himself. We have brief moments of closeness and then we're as far away as ever.'

She hadn't told Grace how she'd wept in his arms. It would only have upset her. But the memory was crystal clear and every time she thought about it she knew that to have him there all the time when she needed comforting would be heaven—if he were only someone other than a Westlake.

'And so where are you going on Friday night?' Davina had asked, bringing her mind back to basics.

Grace had smiled. 'I've got a date.'

'What? You never said.'

'I've only just made the arrangement. I was originally going to go to the cinema, but an American I met on the cruise phoned last night to ask if I would dine with him. He's over here on business and would like to meet up again.'

'And you're going?'

'Yes. He's a very nice man…as Rowan is.'

'Let's hope he hasn't any skeletons in *his* cupboard, then.'

'It's not a romance we're talking about,' Grace had said with deepening colour. 'Just meeting up with a holiday acquaintance.' She'd changed the subject, leaving Davina to wonder why she'd never mentioned the American before.

Rowan was already at his desk when she went in and she flashed him a smile.

'How does it feel?' she asked.

He smiled back.

'The leg? Or being back where I belong?'

'Both.'

'The leg behaved itself reasonably well as I manipulated the stairs, but I'm not ready to run in the hundred metres, or do anything else along those lines just yet. As for being back down here, it's fantastic.'

He was watching her keenly.

'And you, Davina. What about you? Are you all right?'

She'd had to consult him a couple of times about patients' problems since the day he'd held her weeping in his arms, yet neither of them had mentioned it since. But now he was referring to it in an oblique sort of way and she felt compelled to say something.

'I'm sorry about what happened that day in the apartment. It just came over me and I couldn't hold it back.'

'For goodness' sake, Davina!' he breathed. 'You don't have to apologise for your grief. I understood. Even the strongest of us have our moments of despair.'

His eyes were warm, his mouth kind, and she held her breath for what she hoped was coming next. It was one of those moments between them that came out of the blue and made her realise what she would be missing if she shut this man out of her life.

She wanted to tell him that she'd wept that day for them, not her mother. But as if on cue there was a knock on the door and Rosemary, one of the receptionists, came in with an armful of patients' records.

When she began to discuss practice matters with him Davina excused herself and went to get her own day under way, with the feeling that maybe the intervention had been timely.

From the moment of their first meeting her relationship with Rowan had galloped along, until she'd discovered who he was. But now she needed to set her own pace and there was no way she wanted to be swept off her feet a second time until she was sure she could handle it.

When Davina arrived home from the practice on Thursday evening Grace was on the point of leaving. The table in the dining room was set with fine cutlery and glassware beneath the flickering light of candles, and the food was keeping warm on a hostess trolley beside it.

It was a quarter past six and Rowan had arranged to be there by half past seven as, like herself, he would need to shower and change after a day amongst germs and infections.

The American Grace was dining with was called Wesley Barnett and he came from Texas.

'What time is the Dallas cowboy picking you up,' Davina asked with a smile as she stripped off for the shower.

'He's not,' was the reply. 'I'm driving to meet him. I didn't want us to be under your feet when Rowan arrives.'

'He's not due for another hour,' Davina told her.

'Nevertheless,' Grace said firmly, 'I'm not risking anything spoiling your evening. So I'm off...and I won't be in until late. Get the message?'

Davina sighed. 'Don't get your hopes up too high. Rowan and I have a history of rubbing each other up the wrong way.'

'Not this time,' her aunt said confidently, and off she went.

It was half past seven and Rowan hadn't arrived, but Davina wasn't worried. For one thing he wasn't moving around as fast as she was these days, with his leg having only just healed. Or perhaps someone at the surgery had delayed him. So she checked the food to make sure it wasn't drying up and waited.

By eight o'clock she was having her doubts and by half past was beginning to feel let down. She was hungry—ravenous, in fact—having had nothing to eat since a quick sandwich in her lunch-hour.

He couldn't have forgotten, she kept telling herself. Earlier in the day he'd said, 'I'll see you tonight. Is seven thirty all right?'

'Yes, of course,' she'd told him, 'and by the way, Grace sends her apologies. She won't be there. A friend she met on the cruise has asked her out.'

'I see,' he'd said slowly, 'So it will be just you and I.'

'Er…yes. Is that all right?'

He'd smiled. 'Of course.'

But now it wasn't 'all right' at all. A phone call was the obvious thing. If he answered she would find out what was keeping him…and if he didn't she would know he was on his way. Or would she? Supposing he'd slipped on those treacherous stairs. Or something else just as serious had happened. Why hadn't he *rung* her!

There was no answer when she phoned and, with gloom descending increasingly, she settled down to wait with a hunk of bread and a piece of cheese to take away the hunger pangs.

Rowan was ready by a quarter to seven and knowing it was only a ten-minute drive to Heatherlea, and not wanting to appear too eager, he decided to go for a brief spin over the moors above the valley.

It was a warm fine evening, and after the confines of recent weeks he had a sudden yearning for the wide open spaces that he loved just as much as the valley folk did.

High on the flat plateau where sheep roamed wild and windberries ripened ready for late summer gathering, he let out a sigh of sheer pleasure. He was happy. Happier than he'd been in weeks. He was back on the job for one thing, and for another, more important still, Davina was beginning to warm towards him again. She wouldn't have invited him to dinner if she wasn't. Maybe tonight they could make up for lost time.

As he drove round a bend in the road he had to brake sharply. A man in hiker's attire was lying just a few feet away beneath a steep overhanging outcrop of rock.

There was no one else in sight and as Rowan stopped the car and went towards him he was conscious that this was a remote place. It was some miles from the village and if there were any farms or private houses in the area, he didn't know where they were.

The man was moaning softly when Rowan reached him and he saw immediately that there were head and neck injuries and his hands were badly cut. It looked as if he'd fallen over the edge of the outcrop onto the road below and might have been there for some time.

He felt cold and clammy and was shivering uncontrollably. He had to get him to hospital fast, Rowan thought. Fishing his mobile phone out of his jacket pocket, he dialled the number for the emergency services.

There was no answer and he tried again and again. Drat! he thought. They were too far away from the transmitter and he daren't risk trying to get the man into his car. From the look of him his injuries were extensive. Paramedics with a stretcher were needed. So the first vehicle that came along was going to have to go for help.

Hurrying back to his car, he grabbed his bag off the back seat and returned to the injured hiker, whose breathing was shallow, his pulse faint. If he went into cardiac arrest it would be the fellow's lucky day that he himself had been on hand to attempt to resuscitate him.

As he looked anxiously up and down the road for any signs of life, he knew that out there it could be long minutes before anything on wheels came along.

He'd covered the man with his jacket and a rug that he carried in the back of the car, but he wasn't getting any warmer and, apart from giving him a painkilling injection, there wasn't much he could do except wait.

At last a big truck appeared on the horizon and Rowan stepped into the road and flagged it down.

'I've got a seriously injured man here,' he told the driver. 'I'm a doctor and am doing what I can for him, but we need an ambulance urgently and my mobile won't work up here. Can you stop at the next property you come across and get the emergency services up here?'

'Sure thing, Doc,' the man said. 'Leave it to me. I'll put my foot down.' And within seconds the truck was lumbering towards civilisation.

It was forty minutes before an ambulance appeared on the horizon with lights flashing and sirens wailing. The injured man was conscious now and trying to move, but Rowan was urging him to keep still because of the head wounds and the possibility of spinal injuries.

The injection he'd given him was keeping the pain level down for the time being and he was mumbling. 'Turned round to look at a bird, a grouse I think it was. Just then a big black animal jumped out of the bushes. I stepped back and fell over the edge. My wife will wonder where I've got to if I'm not home soon.'

'I'll see that she's informed.' Rowan told him soothingly. 'Just keep still, sir. The ambulance will be here in a moment.'

A vision of Davina eyeing the clock came to mind.

She would be wondering where he'd got to and there was no way he could let her know what had happened while he was stuck out on the moors.

There was a jinx on them, he thought wryly. If he'd gone straight to Heatherlea instead of deciding to go for a quick spin along the tops they would be in the middle of the cosy evening he'd been looking forward to.

The ambulance pulled up and two paramedics spilled out. As they came to kneel beside him one of them asked, 'What happened?'

'He fell over the edge,' Rowan informed them. 'Says some animal jumped out of the bushes and made him lose his footing. I've given him pain relief and kept him still. His pulse was very weak when I found him an hour ago, but it's stronger now that his body's had time to adjust to the shock of the fall.

'He's reasonably lucid. The man is worried about his wife not knowing where he is. Once you've got him inside the ambulance I'll phone her. He's managed to give me the number. But it will have to wait until I get further down the valley. And then I'm going to keep a dinner engagement that I should have turned up for an hour and a half ago.'

When she heard Rowan's car tyres swish to a halt on the drive Davina was on her feet in a flash. She'd been hunched on the sofa in the sitting room, watching television and trying to keep her mind off all the worrying reasons why he hadn't turned up.

The cool, attractive, hostess look she'd intended to present had gone. The long black skirt and white silk top she was wearing were crumpled. The smooth golden cap of her hair was in disarray where she'd raked anxious hands through it, but as she opened the door to him she didn't care.

She was consumed with a mixture of annoyance and anxiety—until she saw the blood down the front of the shirt that he'd painstakingly ironed earlier. The anxiety took over completely then.

His smile was apologetic…and wary.

'What's happened? Where have you been?' she exclaimed as she stepped back to let him in.

'I decided to make a detour on my way here,' he said ruefully. 'I was ready early and, feeling that I needed a short time to myself, I thought I'd go for a quick run over the tops.'

'You mean you needed time to brace yourself for the coming ordeal?'

'No. I don't mean that at all, Davina. I wanted the evening to be a success and needed to clear my mind of any past debris.'

'I see… And what happened?'

He sighed.

'I came across a badly injured hiker. He'd fallen over the edge of a steep rock face and because we were up on the moors I couldn't get through to the emergency services. I had to wait until another vehicle came along and send the driver to get help, all of which was time-consuming.'

'How badly was he injured?' she questioned.

His expression was grave. 'Bad enough. But enough of what I've been up to. What about you? I can imagine what you've been thinking.'

'And what is that?'

'That I'd chickened out.'

'Not really. The thought did cross my mind, but I know you better than that.'

He gave a tired smile.

'Praise at last!'

Davina ignored the amused sarcasm and went on, 'I was more concerned that you might have had another accident and with your leg only recently healed…'

'No. Here I am. Fit and well—and hungry.'

She pulled a wry face.

'Aunt Grace made us a lovely meal but it's somewhat dried up after all this time.'

Rowan looked down at his shirt.

'And I'm not in any fit state to sit down to eat it.'

'We could give it a try. Take your shirt off and I'll put it to soak in cold water to lift the blood stains. Then, while you go up to wash, I'll do what I can to salvage the meal.'

He was observing her with raised eyebrows.

'Are you sure? You don't mind me being only half-dressed while we eat?'

'No,' she said, her eyes warming. 'I don't mind you being half-dressed at all.'

He took off the soiled shirt and a broad, tanned chest and rippling shoulders were revealed. Davina had a sudden aching longing to be held up against him, to be close to the strength and sensual grace of him.

Observing her with the bright hazel gaze that missed nothing, he said, 'The feeling is mutual. You are very beautiful dressed, Davina, but I would imagine that naked you are divine.'

At that moment it was as if there was only the two of them in the world. Everything else that had gone before was forgotten. There was only desire, sweet, demanding desire. A different hunger was in them now. Food was forgotten and, taking his hand, she led him towards the lofty curving staircase.

CHAPTER EIGHT

WHEN they were halfway up the stairs the doorbell rang and they eyed each other ruefully.

'Will that be Grace?' Rowan asked.

Davina shook her head.

'No. She would let herself in, and in any case she said she wouldn't be back until late.'

'So ignore it.'

'Yes, I will.'

It rang again and she made the mistake of glancing through the landing window.

'It's the police!' she exclaimed. 'Jim Gardiner, the village bobby, is down there. I can see the top of his helmet and his bike's propped up against the hedge. I hope that Aunt Grace is all right. She'd gone to meet this man she met on the cruise.'

She was reluctantly withdrawing her hand from his clasp and he sighed.

'You'd better see what he wants, Davina. I'll wait up here.'

'Ah, Davina,' the constable said when she opened the door. 'Sorry to disturb you. I'm trying to track down Dr Westlake. His place is in darkness and I wondered if he'd been called out or anything like that.'

'He's here, Jim,' she said tonelessly, acutely aware that the evening was continuing to be a frustrating affair. 'Dr Westlake was due to dine here earlier but he was delayed by an accident and has just gone upstairs to get cleaned up. If you'd like to step inside I'll fetch him. There's nothing wrong at the surgery, I hope?'

'No, nothing like that,' he said. 'I want to talk to him about the accident.'

When she went back upstairs Rowan was hovering on the landing.

'What does he want?' he asked exasperatedly.

'It's about the accident,' she told him, smiling in spite of the irritating interruption. 'I've covered for the fact that you're only half-dressed by telling him that you're having to get cleaned up after it.'

'A few seconds later and you would have had to think of something better than that,' he replied, adding with a sepulchral groan, 'Can it be that the curse of the Westlakes is still on me?'

Davina had to laugh. 'Go and do your suave doctor bit with the constable and I'll go and see just how far the food is past its peak.'

There was answering amusement in the dark eyes meeting hers. '"Peak" is not a word I want to hear at this moment. If I hadn't gone up amongst them tonight none of this would have happened.'

Davina was serious now.

'True, and that poor man might have died if you hadn't come across him. So if the fates are as usual not on our side, at least they were on his.'

'So what was that all about?' she asked when Rowan came into the kitchen after the constable had gone.

'The police wanted to know if I saw anything suspicious when I was with the injured hiker.'

'Suspicious?'

'He told me that some sort of animal had jumped out at him, causing him to fall over the edge. I didn't see anything myself but was too concerned about his injuries to take particular notice. I told the paramedics what he'd said and they must have informed the police. I thought at the time that the fellow was perhaps disorientated after the fall, but the amazing thing is the constable says that a big cat has been sighted, roaming the moors, and they are warning walkers and local people to be on their guard.

'He came to ask if I'd seen anything suspicious while I'd been with the accident victim but, like I said, I was more concerned with his injuries than the cause of them.'

'So is it a case of "Watch out, watch out, there's a puma about"?' she said with a shudder, looking out into the dark night.

'Why a puma?'

'That's what they usually say it is when a big cat is sighted in moorland areas.'

He laughed.

'That sounds a bit far-fetched. It's probably some-body's outsize tabby.'

'I'm going to dish out what's left of the food,' she told him. 'We may as well eat.'

'And that's it? We're not going to take up where we left off?'

Davina smiled across at him.

'I'm not used to making love in cold blood, and after having the police on the doorstep and warnings of wild animals prowling, our special moment has passed.'

As soon as she'd said it she knew it had been stupid to say that she wasn't used to making love in cold blood. She wasn't used to making love under any conditions. It would have been the first time but, needless to say, Rowan couldn't be expected to know that, and he wasn't going to let it pass.

'So I wouldn't have been the first,' he said tightly, as jealousy ripped through him. Yet even as he said it he knew he had no right to judge. Davina was enchanting. It would be amazing if she hadn't had other lovers before him.

As she was about to tell him that he would indeed have been the first, the evening's final frustration was about to present itself. The back door opened and Grace came in.

'I know I'm earlier than I said I would be,' she told her apologetically, 'but Wes is flying back tomorrow and he has an early start in the morning.'

Her glance went to Rowan standing shirtless at the opposite end of the kitchen, and if Davina hadn't been so fed up she might have laughed at the construction her aunt would be putting on that. Little did she know that an injured hiker, the village constable and a feline-type prowler had all put paid to her plans for the evening.

As if Rowan was reading her thoughts, he said, 'I'll be off, Davina. I can pick up some fish and chips on my way home. Maybe another time, eh?' And with a smile for Grace he went.

'Rowan was in a hurry to depart,' Grace said, taking in Davina's downcast expression. 'Didn't the night go well?'

Davina dredged up a wry smile. 'Not really. As you can see, we've not eaten anything. Rowan decided to go for a drive before he made his way here and came across an injured hiker on the moors. He'd fallen down a rockface and hurt himself badly. It wasn't possible to phone for help as mobile phone reception was too bad, and he had to wait until another driver came along to go for assistance. All of which made him very late getting here.

'Then Jim Gardiner came to ask if Rowan had seen anything suspicious while he was with the hiker as the man was saying that some large animal had jumped out of the bushes and startled him, causing him to take a step back which had resulted in him falling over the edge. Jim said there'd been a few sightings up on the moors of some big animal prowling around and it looked like a big cat of some sort.'

Grace was listening in astonishment.

'Good gracious! The moment I turn my back all sorts of things start happening, and none of them very welcome by the sound of it. Then I add the finishing touch to a disappointing evening by coming home early.'

'It was spoilt long before that,' Davina told her, thinking back to the moment when their progress up the staircase had been halted by the ringing of the doorbell.

'So you didn't get to know Rowan any better?'

'No. Though maybe it was just as well. When we're together it's as if an electric current is passing between us.'

'And you don't want to get burnt? The more I see of him, the more I like him. He's a good man, Davina. Don't blame him for what his father did.'

'I don't any more. But meeting Rowan hasn't been like getting to know any other very attractive man. There's been a blight on our relationship right from the start, which is not surprising.'

'Have you decided whether you're going to keep to what you said about leaving the practice?'

'No. I don't want to. Yet neither do I want to spend the rest of my working life with someone who is so near, yet so far off being the right one for me.'

'Only you know the answer to that,' Grace said sombrely.

'I should, but I don't,' Davina said dismally, and as if that left nothing more to be said they went to bed.

But sleep wasn't easy to come by. As Davina tossed restlessly beneath the covers the evening's happenings were racing around her mind. There'd been her anxiety and annoyance when Rowan hadn't arrived. Then the relief when he had. Only to be followed by dismay when she'd heard the reason for the delay.

Yet all of that hadn't stopped them from being so aware of each other they'd gravitated towards the bedroom. Only to be stopped in their tracks by the constable's visit. After that the magic had fled and there'd been no chance of it rekindling as Grace had come home early.

Rowan was expecting her to be divine naked, she thought as her blood warmed. Would she be? And would he ever see her like that? Not the way things were going. She threw back the sheets and, going to stand in front of the mirror, let her nightgown drop to the floor.

The ache was back. The need to feel him close. But there was no point in going along that road. They'd had their moment and it had been taken from them.

As she stood there in lissom nakedness she was remembering how she'd made matters worse by giving Rowan the impression she'd slept with other men.

It wasn't true. He *would* have been the first, and when a chance came along she would tell him so. With gloom still upon her she pulled the soft cotton shift back over her head and went to the window. As she peered anxiously into the blackness of the night it was easy to imagine that eyes glowing like hot coals were watching her from the bushes.

She returned to her bed determined that there would be only one thought in mind…sleep. And at last, miraculously, it came.

If Davina had intended having a quick word with Rowan before surgery the next morning, it had been a vain hope.

The waiting room was full. Lucy hadn't turned up, having picked up some sort of bug. And the village bobby was creating a lot of interest amongst those waiting with a notice he was putting up that asked the public to be on their guard against a wild animal that was prowling the moors.

'Are you sure it's not the hound of the Baskervilles, Jimbo?' somebody asked jokingly. 'Or Lassie?'

'The moors are full of wild animals,' someone else said, and the constable eyed them sternly.

'This is a serious matter. There have been several sightings and those who've seen the animal say that it looks like a puma.'

As the two doctors made their way to their consulting rooms Rowan said, 'It sounds as if you might have been right.'

'I only said that because something similar occurred when I was small and everyone thought it was a puma.'

'And was it?'

'They never caught it. I think it was just the imaginings of village folk who'd seen a big cat.'

He paused outside the door of his room and with his hand on the handle said, 'Nevertheless, take care, Davina.'

They were chatting as if the night before had never been, she thought, but there was a tightness about him this morning. He was pleasant enough but she sensed tension in him and wasn't surprised. After the frustrations they'd experienced and her stupid comment regarding her love life, he was hardly likely to be full of the joys of spring.

They were alone at that moment in the deserted passage outside the consulting rooms and she thought that here was the moment she'd been waiting for. A chance to explain that she didn't sleep around. But no sooner had the intention been born than one of the receptionists was bearing down on them, asking for an urgent repeat prescription for a patient, and the opportunity was lost.

One of those waiting to consult her was Albert Golightly, one of her father's few friends and, once he was seated opposite, the retired butcher lost no time in describing his problem.

'I keep having funny turns, Davina,' he said with gruff awkwardness, 'which is not like me at all.'

'Tell me about them,' she said with a smile that was meant to make him feel more relaxed.

'I go all sick and dizzy and my legs buckle under me. It only lasts a few seconds, but it's not nice. I keep thinking I'm going to have a stroke.'

'So let's check your blood pressure, shall we?' she suggested.

'It's fine,' she told him as she took the strapping off his arm.

'Right,' he muttered, 'but there has to be a reason for what's happening.'

'Quite so,' she agreed, feeling his neck and cranium with gentle fingers. 'It could be that something is momentarily stopping the blood getting to the brain.'

'My neck does feel strange sometimes.'

'I'm going to give you a note to take to the hospital to have your neck X-rayed,' she told him, 'and if I'm not satisfied with the results from that I'll ask for an MRI scan of the head and the top of the spine. Do you take aspirin?'

'Yes. I take a mild dosage every day.'

'Good. Keep up with that.'

When she'd given him the note for the hospital he got

slowly to his feet and, looking down at her, said, 'Your father would be proud of you.'

'Do you think so?' she said with a wry smile.

Her father's approval of anything at all had always been grudgingly given. In this instance she knew that Albert was referring to the job. Her dour parent would be turning over in his grave if he knew that his daughter was in love with a Westlake. There would be no approval whatsoever with regard to that.

When the waiting room had finally emptied and the two doctors came out of their rooms, Davina waylaid Rowan and suggested casually, 'Do you fancy a bite before we start on the house calls?'

Rowan was still looking a bit tight around the jawline but his reply was easy enough.

'Yes, if you like. Where?'

'The pub.'

'OK. But we'll have to make it brief. We've both got plenty of home visits to do.'

Once they were seated at a table with sandwiches and coffee in front of them Davina said, 'I feel really bad about last night, Rowan.'

'You have no cause to,' he told her unsmilingly. 'I was the one who messed things up. If I hadn't given in to the lure of the moors none of it would have happened.'

'You were doing what you're pledged to do, helping the sick,' she said levelly, with the feeling that words were being left unsaid. 'And the constable's visit and Aunt Grace's early return were just the fates finishing off what they'd started with the injured hiker.'

'When I said I felt bad about last night it wasn't for those reasons. It was because I let you go home hungry...and gave you the impression that I slept around.'

'You don't have to answer to me for what you do in

your life, Davina,' he said in a low voice. 'You're young and very beautiful. It would be amazing if other men hadn't wanted you. I'm right there amongst them. But I'm a different kettle of fish, aren't I? I'm a Westlake. I feel that ever since we met there's been a jinx on us, which is not surprising. And though last night might have been a disaster in one way, in another it might have been our salvation.

'You are free to choose any man you want and unless he's already married or a fool, he will come running. So why settle for me? Someone who comes with the trappings of the past?'

'I can't believe you're saying this,' she said dismally. 'Just as I've finally come to terms with who you are, *you're* having doubts. Am I to take it that you're suggesting we cool it?'

'I don't know what I'm suggesting,' he told her grimly. 'For one thing, I still don't know if you're intending moving on now that I'm back in harness.'

'I haven't made up my mind about that.'

As if she hadn't spoken, he went on, 'And if you do carry out your threat, what's the point? We would never see each other. And it would prove that you *haven't* accepted me for who I am. Let's face it, I haven't brought much joy into your life so far.'

'That's not to say it wouldn't happen in the future, and there are other ingredients just as important, like sexual chemistry, integrity, compatibility, trust.'

'Trust!' he hooted. 'I wouldn't have thought that came high on the list. Not after the way I…how was it you described it? Sneaked into your life.'

This was the moment to tell Rowan that the two of them were all that mattered. That without him she was lost. But the words wouldn't come. He was making excuses, condemning himself out of his own mouth, and it could only be for one reason. He wanted out of the situation that was developing between them and if that wasn't humiliating she didn't know what was.

She got to her feet. 'You've made your point. I've got the message. I'll see you back at the practice.' And before he could say anything further she walked away without a backward glance.

As Rowan watched her drive off he thought achingly that Davina was a modern woman with the values of a bygone age. Her eagerness to put the record straight from the night before had made his resolve weaken, especially as he remembered how she'd been ready to give herself to *him*.

But what had he done? Twisted her words into an escape route, when all he wanted was to take her in his arms and never let her go. He'd never condemned his father for what had happened all that time ago, but he cursed him for having put the burden of his sins onto himself.

As he'd eaten his solitary supper the night before he'd felt as if a great weight had been settling on him. It had been as Davina had described it. Just as she was coming to terms with who he was, *he* was the one having doubts.

He was so afraid of hurting her. Of giving her children that would bear a name that was besmirched with bad memories. What he'd just said to her had sounded like words of wisdom issuing forth, but now he thought they'd been the gabblings of a fool. If they really loved each other, what did anything else matter?

Muriel Pearson lived in a remote farm on the tops. She was a friend of Grace and when Davina had been small they'd often gone to visit. There'd always been a warm welcome and a plate of goodies waiting for her and she hadn't forgotten.

That had been in the days when the farm had been a thriving concern, but after Muriel's husband had died the livestock had been sold off and now there remained just a few chickens.

When she opened the door to Davina, the elderly widow exclaimed, 'Davina! You shouldn't have to be coming all the way up here again. I'm all right now.'

Putting her arm around Muriel's bony shoulders, Davina hugged her. 'I'll be the judge of that,' she told her chidingly, and while Muriel bustled into the kitchen to put the kettle on she got out her stethoscope.

Muriel had been discharged from hospital recently after a bout of pneumonia and Davina was concerned about her, but today she was relieved to find that her chest and lungs were clear.

'So what's going on in the village,' the elderly widow asked as she buttoned her blouse. 'I hear you've got a new doctor at the practice in Andrew Swinburn's place.'

'Yes, we have,' Davina told her. She took a deep breath. 'His name is Rowan Westlake.'

'Westlake!' Muriel exclaimed, almost dropping the teapot. 'He's not connected with..?'

'I'm afraid so. He's Owen Westlake's son.'

'Bless my soul!' Muriel breathed. 'They do say that the mills of God turn slow, but really! It must be twenty years since your Ma left. What's brought him to the valley?'

'He came to find me. To tell me that my mother was killed in a car crash on the day she left here…and to introduce himself as the new doctor. Though not in that order. He'd been at the practice for a few weeks before he told me who his father was.'

With her amazement unabated, the old lady said, 'He sounds a bit of an upstart. Why didn't he seek you out before?'

'He didn't even know that my mother had a daughter until recently. His father told him just before he died.'

'Well, he can't be blamed for that, then.'

Rowan can't be blamed for anything, Davina thought. Except maybe for enchanting her to the point where she knew she would never ever feel the same about any other man.

But she hadn't come to burden Muriel with her problems.

'How is everything here?' she asked with a smile and a change of subject. 'Are the chickens still laying?'

Muriel nodded.

'Yes. I've got some eggs for you and Grace.'

When it was time to go she came to the door to say goodbye and as Davina's glance went over the garden she saw that it was all churned up, with plants in disarray and bushes flattened.

'What's happened to the garden?' she asked. 'I'll come and help you to get it straight if you like.'

She tried to sound casual knowing how independent Muriel was, and wasn't surprised when the elderly widow shook her head.

'No. You've enough to do. I've asked one of the teenage lads from the next farm to tidy it up for me. It had got left a bit with my being poorly, but it wasn't that bad until the other night when there was something threshing about during the small hours. When I got up the next morning this is how it was.'

'A walker was injured yesterday,' Davina told her. 'He fell over a rock-face due to what he said was an animal jumping out at him. The police are saying it might be a puma.'

'We've heard that before, haven't we?' Muriel said dubiously. 'But it never came to anything.'

'Just the same, take care,' Davina warned.

Muriel smiled. 'I'll have to get the shotgun out. And you had better be on your way. Or that Westlake fellow will be after you. What's he like?'

It was Davina's turn to smile.

'An excellent doctor, very attractive and unattached.'

'Oh, I see,' Muriel said with a knowing twinkle. 'Well, it wouldn't be history repeating itself, would it? Neither of *you* would be hurting anybody.'

Except maybe ourselves, Davina thought as she picked her way along the untidy path.

Back at the practice she was in serious mood and Rowan said, 'I'm sorry that I've upset you. I should have chosen a more suitable moment.'

He could have added that he was already regretting it, and for her part Davina could have told him that there would never be a right moment for him to tell her he wanted to steer clear of her. But she'd shelved all the dismal thoughts their earlier discussion had brought and was concerned about something else. She shook her head.

'I'm not thinking about us at the moment. I'm worried about Muriel Pearson.'

There was surprise in Rowan's keen dark gaze. 'Why? I thought she was much better.'

'She is. My concerns are about what might be roaming around her place.'

'Not the beast of the moors?'

'I'm not sure. But something has been trampling all over her garden and has more or less wrecked it. It was during the night. She didn't get up to investigate, which is unlike her and shows that she's not as fit as she was, but the next morning the damage was there. She's not afraid. Muriel is a tough old dear, and will have everywhere bolted and barred tonight, but how do we know that the thing won't appear in the daylight? It did for the hiker, didn't it?'

'You don't really think it's a puma, do you?' he asked. 'I mean, where would a beast of that nature come from in these parts?'

'No, not really,' she replied, 'but, Rowan, there is something wandering the moors and it has already caused one person to end up in hospital.'

'So why don't we do a stake-out…you and I?'

She looked at him with wide blue eyes. 'A stake-out!'

'We could take your black car—it's not as conspicuous as my white one—and park ourselves near Muriel's for the night. I know that she's an independent old soul, but she doesn't need to know we're there.'

'And how do we know it will come back to that same spot?'

'We don't, but it's worth a try.'

'So what do we do if we see it?'

'I'll take my camera and while I'm taking a picture of it you can phone the police.' He was laughing. 'I'm not suggesting that we branch into big-game hunting.'

'All right,' she agreed. 'And I'll bring a flask and some sandwiches.'

For the rest of the afternoon there was a smile on her face. A few hours spent with Rowan in the cosy confines of her car would make up in part for last night. Further than that she wasn't going to speculate.

*   *   *

'I'm worried about Muriel,' she told Grace as they ate their evening meal that night.

Her aunt looked at her anxiously. 'Why? Is she ill again?'

'No. Nothing like that. She's much better.'

'So why the concern?'

'Some sort of creature has been rampaging through her front garden and made a complete mess of it.'

'Creature? You don't mean the animal that is making everyone nervous.'

'I don't know, do I? But Rowan has suggested that he and I keep watch tonight to see if it comes back.'

'You can't expect it to return just when you want it to,' Grace protested. 'You could be sitting there all night for nothing.'

'Not exactly for nothing,' Davina told her. 'Rowan has got some idea in his head that we ought to cool it. He thinks that being with him will only bring me misery.'

'And what do you think?'

'He might be right, but I'll certainly be miserable without him. I don't know what the answer is. There's one thing I do know, though. The time we spend on surveillance will be the first chance we've had to really be together for any length of time.'

'And you're going to take advantage of it.'

Davina smiled. 'Something like that.'

'Muriel won't like it if she knows you're fussing.'

'She won't know. We'll keep out of sight.'

'Sounds like a crazy idea,' Grace said dubiously.

'What? My wanting to be with Rowan?'

'No. Expecting this beastie to come just when you want it to. And what are you going to do if it does turn up?'

'Take a photograph of it and phone the police.'

'It's to be hoped they don't send the village bobby on his bike or it will be long gone. I shall go to see Muriel myself tomorrow. It's a while since we had a chat. Does she know that Rowan is a Westlake?'

'She didn't. But she does now.'

'What did she have to say?'

'Not a lot after the first amazement had worn off. But Muriel's a shrewd old thing. She guessed that I was attracted to him.'

'She was always on your mother's side, you know. Knew how unhappy she was, so I don't think she'd have any problems with that. Just the same as I haven't. All we want is to see you happy.'

'And what do I do if the man I'm in love with thinks he won't be able to do that?'

'What?'

'Make me happy.'

'It will be up to you to show him that he can. It doesn't mean that because he brought you bad news, *he's* bad news. It doesn't sound like him, this lack of confidence, but his father put him in a very difficult position when he made him promise to seek you out, and Rowan didn't make it any easier for himself by moving into the village.'

'If he hadn't done so I would never have got to know him. He would have sought me out and gone.'

'And in spite of everything, you wouldn't have wanted to miss that?'

'Definitely not…no matter what happens.'

Grace was smiling. 'Your mother's wedding dress is still hanging in my wardrobe and the style of it has just about come round again.'

'Really? Well, I don't think we need to rush it round to the cleaners just yet…and I take it that you *are* kidding. I wouldn't want to take the risk. It didn't bring her much joy.'

CHAPTER NINE

As DAVINA parked her car in the shadow of a clump of trees in the lane beside Muriel's farmhouse, a full moon looked down from the sky above. It was a warm, mellow night and although she'd brought a jacket in case it got chilly later, for the present she was warm enough in a white sleeveless top and cropped blue denims.

When she'd called for Rowan at half past eleven, he'd said, 'So you haven't changed your mind?'

'No. Of course not. I'm keen to solve the mystery,' she'd told him decisively. 'Aunt Grace thinks we're crazy to expect whatever it is to be there again at Muriel's place, but animals are creatures of habit, aren't they?'

'If you say so,' he'd said with an absent smile, his mind on other things.

He'd had a phone call from Carlotta earlier, asking to see him on a doctor-patient basis on Monday, and it had put a dampener on the evening.

She was living and working in Manchester, he'd commented when she'd explained why she was calling, so why not consult a doctor there?

'I'd have thought the reason was obvious,' she'd snapped pettishly. 'You know me better than most people.'

She wasn't wrong about that, he'd thought grimly. For a brief space of time, when he hadn't been thinking straight, he'd thought she was good fun. Only to realise that 'fun' was what she was about and her idea of it didn't always coincide with his.

'So what time can you see me?' she'd persisted.

'Er…make it midday,' he'd said. 'After morning surgery as you're not a patient of the practice.'

And then Davina had arrived looking cool and beautiful. As his heartbeat had quickened at the sight of her he'd thought that no matter how often she tried to intrude into his life, Carlotta was the past. While Davina could be the future if only he could rid himself of the guilt that had been foisted on him. He'd already upset her once today. Best to let the night pass in friendly camaraderie and take it from there.

He'd put Carlotta out of his thoughts as Davina had driven them up the hill road towards Muriel's farm, and by the time she parked the car his mood was lightening.

His suggestion that they should involve themselves in this vigil on the darkened hillside had been in direct contradiction to what he'd said earlier regarding cooling their relationship. He thought that she must be wondering if he knew his own mind. The truth of it was that he didn't, and indecision always sat uncomfortably upon him.

As she switched off the engine and the lights, so that the only illumination was the light of the moon, he said, 'Let's move to the back seat. It will be more comfortable if either of us wants to sleep while the other keeps watch.'

Davina nodded. The suggestion was appealing but his manner was crisp and businesslike. She hoped he wasn't going to use the opportunity to discuss practice matters. It was a chance to talk about themselves, their feelings, hopes and dreams, and in the confines of her car there would be an intimacy they hadn't shared before.

The midsummer day was drawing to a close. It was almost midnight and once they'd settled themselves in the back seat she turned towards him. Her face was in shadow but her teeth gleamed whitely and the honey gold of her hair shone in the moon's light. She was leaning forward. Her perfume was light and tantalising. Rowan could see the cleft between her breasts above the low-cut neck of the top she was wearing and he groaned inwardly.

He'd been consumed with longing from the moment Davina had arrived at the apartment and now it was a burning ache inside him. But with the memory of what he'd said earlier in the day still crystal clear, he didn't take advantage of the moment.

Davina could sense the desire in him as if it were a tangible thing and she thought that never before had she been able to tune into anyone's emotions as she was tuned into his. But she'd been warned off and instead of responding she said casually, 'I would imagine that this is the last thing you would have expected to be doing when you moved into the valley.'

'This and others,' he replied dryly. 'For example, I never expected to fall in love with the young doctor I would be working with and who might have been my stepsister if things had worked out differently. Andrew told me he had a young woman trainee GP working with him and I agreed that she should stay on if she wished, but no names had been mentioned otherwise I might have thought twice about coming here.

'When I promised to carry out my father's last wish I saw myself as merely the messenger. I never expected the woman I'd come to find to be so enchanting.'

'So you're saying that you *do* love me, but deep down you wish you didn't,' she said with unconscious wistfulness.

'Yes, something like that, Davina. You've been generous enough to forgive my duplicity when I first came here, but it doesn't stop me from doubting if I could make you happy in the long term.'

She had drawn away from him and was huddled in the farthest corner of the seat.

'Why do I feel that you're making excuses?'

'Excuses!' he bellowed. 'Do you think I enjoy holding back when all I want to do is this?'

He'd reached out for her and as his arms went round her she melted into bliss. His kisses were like the man, mesmerising, his hold on her that of the lover she wanted him to be. They would have gone on to make love there and then in the back seat of the car with Rowan's concerns on her behalf put to one side, but the animal world had other plans.

A dark shape was lumbering past the car with none of the feline grace of the cat family, and as they brought their minds back to the reason they were there Rowan said, 'That's a young bullock taking a midnight stroll if I'm not mistaken.'

'Yes,' she breathed, 'and it's making straight for Muriel's garden. She must have something growing there that it likes the taste of.'

Rowan was already out of the car ready to give chase and when she joined him he said, 'Let's see if we can persuade it to leave without disturbing her.'

It was too late. As they reached the garden gate the light went on in the hall of the farmhouse and the next second the elderly widow was framed in the doorway, shouting to the offending animal to be on its way.

'Who's there?' she called on seeing them in the shadows, and they saw that she was holding a shotgun.

The bullock was turning, ready to beat a retreat, and as they stepped back to let it pass Davina called, 'It's

Davina and Dr Westlake, Muriel. I was worried about you and we've been keeping watch.'

'You'd better come in for a cup of tea, then,' Muriel said with a dry chuckle, 'now that we know what's been wreaking havoc in my garden.'

'Do we have to?' Rowan whispered in mock horror. 'Does Muriel know what she's doing with the gun? Has she got a licence?'

'Of course she has,' Davina told him laughingly. 'Most of the farmers round here carry shotguns for vermin and self-protection, as some of them live in very remote areas…even more lonely than this. Come on, Rowan, it's the least we can do. I would imagine that seeing us hovering at the gate scared her more than the midnight marauder.'

'That young bullock will be from the next farm. It'll belong to the folks whose lad is helping me tidy the garden,' Muriel said as the three of them sat with mugs of hot tea. 'They're a slapdash lot. Don't keep an eye on the livestock as they should. I shall have a word with them in the morning. One can't blame the beast if it's allowed to roam where it will.'

'At least it wasn't a puma,' Rowan said. 'I don't think we've solved anything with regard to that. No one is going to mistake a frisky young bullock for a big cat. Whatever it is must still be around.'

Muriel was observing him thoughtfully with shrewd grey eyes and Davina found she was holding her breath. If she had something to say, the elderly widow would say it. She'd never been known to mince words.

'I've been wanting to meet you, Dr Westlake,' she said. 'Though I never expected to make your acquaintance under these circumstances. I'm told that you're kin to the fellow who took Davina's mother from her.'

Davina closed her eyes and swallowed hard.

'I don't think this is the moment to be bringing that up, Muriel,' she said, dreading having to meet Rowan's glance.

'It's all right, Davina,' he said levelly. He turned to Muriel. 'Yes. I am related to Owen Westlake. He was my father.'

'So I'm told,' she countered, and then, to Davina's increasing dismay, she went on, 'You look to be a fine upstanding young fellow, but handsome is as handsome does. Whatever made you decide to settle in these parts? The folks in this valley had to watch this girl grow up without a mother and we wouldn't like to see you bring any further hurt into her life.'

Rowan was on his feet and looking down at Muriel's sparse frame, with all expression wiped from his face he said, 'I'll bear that in mind, Mrs Pearson, and with regard to you wanting to know why I chose this part of the country to set up practice, I really don't know. I was drawn to it for some reason. I came up north to take my degree and found the rugged Pennines more appealing than the more mellow uplands of my native Sussex.'

'And now, if you have no further warnings to pass on, I think that Davina and I should be making tracks, as our having been up half the night won't make any difference to the numbers waiting to consult us in the morning.'

As Muriel slid the bolts into place behind them, Davina followed Rowan down the garden path. She was numb with dismay and embarrassment.

For two evenings on the run they'd had their time together spoilt by someone else. Yesterday the hiker and the constable had been responsible, and tonight first the wandering bullock and then Muriel with her sharp tongue and keen sense of injustice had fragmented their privacy.

But in Muriel's case it had been she who had been unjust. Tarring Rowan with the same brush as his father. Yet Davina knew why Muriel had spoken as she had. It had been out of affection and concern for herself. The old lady wasn't to know that Rowan didn't need reminding about her mother and his father, that he was already having doubts about the wisdom of where the two of them were heading.

They were almost home before either of them spoke. Davina was desperately searching for the right words, having no desire to make matters worse. What thoughts were in Rowan's mind she had no idea. Yet they couldn't separate like this. She had to say something.

'I'm so sorry about what Muriel said,' she told him at last. 'She had no right to take you to task like that.'

He'd been staring straight ahead, but now he turned to face her.

'She had every right,' he said dryly. 'The woman cares about you. They all do. It's a wonder they've not had me in the stocks before now. It's like I said this morning, Davina, I've not brought you much joy so far and can't see how that is going to change.'

'Please, don't talk like that,' she begged. 'It's how *I* feel that counts and I think I've made it clear enough.'

Rowan shook his head. 'Subject closed. Consider that Muriel did you a favour.' As she stopped the car in front of the stone facade of the practice, he added, 'Take care, Davina.'

'Let me come up for a moment,' she pleaded. 'We can't leave each other like this.'

He shook his head again.

'We have to. Remember what was going on in the car when the animal appeared. I'm not made of stone,

Davina. If I'm going to put the brake on, the last thing I need is to be alone with you.'

And as she shrank back at the finality of what he was saying he put his key in the lock and went inside.

When she got back to Heatherlea Davina didn't go straight in. She went to the stable and as Jasper neighed his pleasure at the sight of her she told him miserably, 'I wish that Rowan and I were both someone else, Jasper. Thank goodness I've got you and Aunt Grace. The two things in my life that never change.'

'So did you catch the beast of the moors?' Grace called from her bedroom as Davina went slowly up the winding staircase a little later.

'Not exactly,' she replied. 'It was a young bullock that had been trampling around in Muriel's garden. We had a cup of tea with her when it had been sent on its way. In return *she* proceeded to trample over Rowan's feelings.'

'Oh, no!' Grace exclaimed, now out on the landing. 'Yet that is like her. Everything is either black or white where she's concerned, no in-betweens.'

'There's nothing wrong with that if it is justified,' Davina remarked wearily. 'But not in this case.'

'What did Rowan have to say?'

'Not a lot. Just that what she'd said went to confirm what he was already aware of. In other words, we're back to going nowhere.'

'It will sort itself out,' Grace said consolingly. 'You'll see. He'll have calmed down by the next time you see him.'

'That's just it. He *was* calm. Too much so. I'd have been happier if he'd ranted and raved.'

*   *   *

While Davina was telling Grace about the happenings out at Muriel's place, Rowan was standing by the window of his sitting room, looking out into the night.

It was true, what he'd told his elderly inquisitor. He didn't really know why he'd decided to live and work in the valley. Maybe the fates had been pulling his strings towards that end, and when he'd met Davina he'd been grateful if they had.

Yet time had shown that it would have been better if he'd gone somewhere else to practise and made the passing on of his father's last message a separate thing. But in his arrogance he'd decided to combine the two…and where had it got him?

He'd ended up in a situation that he had no control over, and he didn't like that. Muriel Pearson had given him a blunt warning and, enchanted as he was with Davina, if he were to follow his heart and ask her to marry him, did he want to spend the rest of his days watching his step? Making sure that no one could accuse him of following in his father's footsteps or hurting her in any other way?

Marriage, in his view, should be on an equal footing. The two participants loving and trusting each other with no strings attached. There would be little chance of that with the eyes of the valley folk on him all the time, watching and waiting for him to put a foot wrong.

He wished now that he'd never suggested they keep watch at the Pearson farm, but if Muriel hadn't put him in his place, no doubt someone else would have done sooner or later.

The night was half over. He was taking the short Saturday morning surgery, but on Monday they would be back in the surgery side by side and at that moment it seemed as if that was going to be the only way they would ever function as a unit. And if Davina kept to her intention of leaving the practice, there wouldn't even be that.

Rowan was already attending his first patient when Davina arrived on Monday morning. Where normally she would have put her head round the door in brief greeting, today she picked up her post and went straight into her own room.

She wasn't looking forward to coming face to face with Rowan again, but there would be no avoiding that, so brisk and businesslike was going to have to be the order of the day when all she wanted to do was throw herself into his arms and tell him that as long as he loved her nothing else mattered.

But she was discovering that Rowan had his pride and it had received a battering ever since his identity had become known. In the first instance there had been her own reaction. But her feelings for him had proved to be stronger than her anger at his intrusion into her life and now she loved him unreservedly.

Yet that didn't seem to matter as far as he was concerned. Rowan was only prepared to see his side of things and he'd taken Muriel's well-intentioned but disastrous comments of the night before as more proof of the unsuitability of any commitment between them.

With half the night spent on the hillside and the catastrophic visit to the farmhouse, she was weary before the day had even got under way, and as she buzzed for her first patient to come in Davina took a deep breath and dredged up a smile.

Janet Telfer was the village librarian. She was due to retire shortly, as was her husband, Frank, and what they were going to do when the time arrived was the one topic of conversation between them. They had no family to concern themselves over and were all set to settle in the sun somewhere abroad.

She was a bubbly, pleasant woman, always helpful and informative in the small library that was part of the council offices, but today Janet had no smiles for Davina.

'It's Frank, Davina,' she said, choking back tears. 'He needs to see a doctor, but I felt I had to speak to you first.'

'So what's the problem?' she asked.

'I think he's starting with Alzheimer's.'

'What makes you think that, Janet?'

'He's behaving strangely and not talking sense.'

'All the time?'

'No. Not all the time, but most of it. Sometimes he doesn't even know who I am.'

'I'll come out to your place as soon as surgery is over. I take it that he's not at work.'

Janet shook her head. They were both aware that her husband's job as an optician required a mind that was not fogged up.

'He only had a couple of months to do before retiring but he couldn't carry on. His lack of concentration and general state of mind would have been putting the public at risk.'

'Frank might have had a slight stroke and this is the effect of it,' Davina suggested.

The worried librarian looked doubtful. 'He's always been careful about his health. Has one of those machines to check his blood pressure whenever he thinks it necessary, eats all the right kind of foods, has always taken plenty of exercise.'

'Let's wait until I've seen him then before we start

jumping to conclusions. Or would you prefer Dr Westlake to see him?'

As Janet hesitated Davina said, 'I'll tell you what. I'll ask him to come with me. We'll both visit Frank.'

'I'd be grateful for that. Frank only sees a doctor when he can't avoid it. If he was his normal self he would hesitate. But the state he's in, he won't even understand why you're there.'

When she'd gone Davina sat deep in thought for a few moments. Asking Rowan to go with her to the immaculate cottage by the side of the church was a good idea…from the patient's point of view. What Rowan would think of the idea could be another matter.

When the last of her patients had taken their leave she went to find him. There was no sound of voices coming from his room so, not sure if it was empty or if he was writing up notes from the cases he'd seen, she knocked once and then pushed back the door to find that neither assumption was correct. The room wasn't empty and Rowan wasn't seated at his desk. He was standing by the window with Carlotta in his arms.

As Davina observed them in mute amazement his eyes met hers above Carlotta's dark ebony tresses. There was a message in them of some sort, but she didn't stay long enough to discover what it was. She'd told Janet Telfer she would ask Rowan to visit with her, but was he going to want to cut short his time with Carlotta? Perhaps he thought there were fewer complications to romancing Carlotta than being entangled with herself.

Some of the staff were eating their lunch in the small kitchen at the back of the practice and, making herself a coffee, Davina sat down with them. She'd been hungry before but now any appetite she'd had was gone and before getting involved in their chatter she drank up quickly and went to check on the number of calls she had to make.

To her surprise Rowan was outside on the forecourt of the surgery, waving Carlotta off, and as her car roared off into the summer afternoon he turned and came back inside to find Davina waiting for him.

'I can explain,' he said with a quick glance at her set face.

'No need,' she told him abruptly. 'I need to speak to you about a different matter. I have a patient whose wife is worried he might have Alzheimer's. She came to see me this morning and I've promised to put him on my list for today. I wondered if you would come with me. I'd value your opinion and so would she.'

'Yes, of course,' he said immediately. 'We'll make it our first call, shall we? Where do these people live?'

'It's the Telfers. They live next door to the church. It's only two minutes' walk away.'

'Give me a shout when you're ready. I have to make a hospital appointment for someone before I do anything else.'

As they walked to the Telfers' cottage Rowan said, 'Aren't you going to ask me what was going on with Carlotta and I when you burst in on us?'

'Burst in on you! You have a cheek. I did what I usually do at the end of surgery, check to see where you are if I have something that I wish to discuss. And I don't feel the need to probe. It was quite obvious what was going on from where I was standing.'

'Was it really?' he said dryly. 'Perhaps you should have taken a closer look.'

'Meaning?'

'She was distressed and I was comforting her.'

'*I* was distressed last night,' she replied coolly, 'but there wasn't any comfort coming *my* way.'

'Yes, but *you* didn't think you might have skin cancer. *Your* only problem was the man in your life…me.'

'Oh! So you *are* still in my life? And what's this about Carlotta having cancer?'

'She's got what might be a basal cell carcinoma on her face.'

'I'm sorry to hear that,' Davina said, immediately contrite. 'It's the last thing someone in the acting profession would want to have, isn't it?'

'It is indeed,' he agreed levelly, and as by then they'd reached the Telfers' house the subject was dropped.

As soon as Davina saw Frank Telfer she knew that something was very amiss. He was shuffling around the room, picking things up and putting them down all the time, and when Janet said, 'The doctors have come to see you, Frank,' he eyed them blankly.

His blood pressure was normal, his heartbeat regular. There were no signs of a stroke, although both doctors knew that there could have been a mild one.

'Before we send your husband to see a neurologist, I want to have some urine tests done,' Rowan told Janet. 'Will you bring a sample to the surgery within the next hour?'

'Yes, of course,' she agreed. 'I'll do anything, anything you say, if only it will make Frank better. Do *you* think it's the start of Alzheimer's, Doctor?'

'I don't want to make a guess,' he told her. 'There are certain features of the disease present, but that is not to say that's what it is. Tell me, has he had any bladder problems recently?'

'There was a prostate problem some time ago,' she said. 'Dr Swinburn treated him for it, but I don't think it cleared up properly. He's still been having a few problems, but with you being new…and Davina being of the opposite sex, he wouldn't come to the surgery.'

Rowan nodded. 'We'll see what the urine tests show up, Mrs Telfer. It could be something totally different from Alzheimer's that is affecting your husband. But don't get too optimistic. Let's get those tests sent off today.'

As they walked back to the surgery Davina said, 'What are you thinking? I've never heard of a bladder problem affecting the mind.'

'Oh, but it can. A urinary tract infection, or urethritis as we medics know it, can cause all sorts of serious complications. Bacteria pass through the urethra into the bladder and the kidneys. If the infection is out of control it can cause septicaemia, or a form of dementia for which some poor folk in less enlightened times might have been sectioned. All it needs is a course of strong antibiotics. It's a long shot, but it's worth following up. Compared to Alzheimer's it's certainly the lesser of two evils. I'm sorry for what I said about Carlotta and you,' she told him as they came to a halt outside the practice. 'She must rely on you a lot to come all this way for a consultation.'

'I don't know about that,' he said with a wry smile. 'Carlotta is a devious woman. She usually has a hidden agenda of some sort. But in this instance I couldn't help but feel sorry for her. The blemish does look like a basal cell carcinoma and her looks mean everything to her. But as we both know, that should be the least of her worries. The main thing is to get it removed and keep a close watch for any further symptoms. It's nice to know I'm forgiven for one thing,' he went on, with the smile still tugging at his mouth, and Davina felt annoyance surfacing.

'There's no need to sound so put upon,' she remonstrated. 'If you're referring to what happened on Friday night, your repeat performance of putting me in my place, that's your problem. If anyone should be putting up the barriers it's me. But I've decided that I'm going to get on with my life and if you're prepared to sit up there on your pedestal and watch me, again that's your problem.'

On that note of defiance she marched out on her rounds.

In the week that followed Rowan didn't have any comment to make about Davina's outburst so she could only conclude that nothing had changed. He was determined to stay at a distance as far as their personal lives were concerned, and he wasn't exactly forever at her elbow in the surgery either.

She was feeling low-spirited and rejected, but there were a few things to rejoice over. For one thing, the tests had shown that Frank Telfer was indeed suffering from a deep-seated urinary tract infection. He had been admitted to hospital and was being given intravenous antibiotics.

There had been an immediate improvement both mentally and physically, and Janet could once more see their Spanish villa beckoning now that the threat of Alzheimer's was receding.

There'd been good news regarding Carlotta's skin problem, too. It had been cancerous but when the rodent ulcer was removed there were no signs of it having spread.

Grace was also having her share of good news. Her American friend was due over on business again soon and, noting her aunt's delight at the prospect, Davina had to accept that there might be romance in the air.

The only one who hadn't got anything pleasurable going on in their life was herself, and every time she saw Rowan she thought dismally that he was to blame for that.

He was paler and thinner these days. She caught him wincing a couple of times, as if his leg was still tender, but when she would have asked if it was bothering him his unrelenting jawline made her hesitate.

Yet he was pleasant enough most of the time. When she and Grace were in the pub one night at the same time as he was, he bought them a drink and chatted for a while. But it was all surface talk and when he'd gone Grace said ruefully, 'What is that man trying to prove?'

'He's either too honourable for his own good, or he's using our situation as an excuse,' Davina said glumly. 'Maybe he's one of those men who aren't in the market for marriage. Who don't want the responsibility of it. And let's face it, for anyone reluctant to take the step, in a situation like ours he would already be at a disadvantage.'

Grace looked at her anxiously. Unrequited love wasn't what she wanted for Davina. Yet it wasn't quite like that. Rowan Westlake *was* in love with her niece. One had only to look at him when he was near her. So why was he putting them both through this?

She'd told her friend Muriel to watch what she said in future. That Rowan wasn't responsible for his father's misdeeds and that Davina was in love with him.

'That doesn't surprise me,' the old stalwart had said, 'and if this doctor fellow is as special as you both think he is, it's up to him to do something about it.'

'He might have done if you hadn't put your oar in,' Grace had told her in affectionate exasperation and had left it at that.

*   *   *

That night Rowan stayed in the pub long after they'd left. He didn't want to go home to the silent apartment. He knew that lots of men wouldn't have given a second thought to the things that plagued *him*. He didn't understand why he was being so indecisive. If Davina had been anyone else, he would have been proud to ask her to take his name and would be looking forward to passing it on to their children.

What was in a name, for heaven's sake? It shouldn't matter, but it did.

CHAPTER TEN

As THE golden days of summer shortened into autumn and Davina's relationship with Rowan continued to falter, Grace's friendship with Wesley Barnett was blossoming into romance.

He'd been over again from Texas and Davina had insisted that this time he stay at Heatherlea.

'Are you sure?' her aunt had questioned. 'This is *your* home, Davina.'

'It might be, legally,' she'd replied, 'but as far as I'm concerned Heatherlea is *ours*. It's your home as much as mine, Aunt Grace. So do, please, ask Wes to come and stay.'

She'd liked the bluff Texan widower immediately. Loved the way he doted on Grace. Watching how her aunt had sparkled when he'd been around, she'd begun to hear wedding bells in the distance.

Grace had gone back to Texas with him for a visit. Wes had wanted her to see his ranch and meet his family, and when she'd returned there'd been a diamond on her finger.

Blushing like a schoolgirl, she said, 'Am I being a silly old fool, Davina?'

'No, my darling aunt, you are not!' Davina told her firmly. 'If you love each other as much as I think you do, don't hesitate. Don't let it all be spoilt because one of you has too much pride, too little faith, or whatever. Do it.'

Grace's face clouded.

'If I did decide not to marry Wesley, there would be different reasons than those stopping me,' she'd said. 'How can I go to live so far away and leave you alone and miserable? If everything was all right with Rowan and you, it would be different, but it isn't, is it? And I can't expect Wes to move over here. His livelihood is in Texas. He has a son and daughter and grandchildren out there, too.'

Davina hugged her aunt.

'I could always be with you in a matter of hours. It's not as if we would never see each other again. Tomorrow we'll go to buy wedding outfits,' she told her firmly. 'And by the way, where is the wedding going to be? Here or in Texas?'

'Here. I want to be married amongst the Pennines, in the place where I've spent most of my life. If I'm going to live over there, Wesley will have to come here for the wedding.'

'Heatherlea is just made for it,' Davina crowed. 'We could get outside caterers in. Fill the house with flowers and it would be a perfect background for photographs.'

Her doubts fading after her niece's convincing display of delight, Grace's sparkle came back, and when Davina asked what colour she'd thought of wearing she said, 'Pale blue, I think. And what about you…my bridesmaid?'

'Oh, I think I've got an old frock I can jazz up.' Davina teased, and went to take afternoon surgery in a more sombre mood than the one she'd presented to Grace. Big changes were taking place in her life. It had started when Rowan Westlake had butted into it and it was going on from there.

But of one thing she was sure. Grace deserved this

chance of happiness and not one word would pass her own lips to make her aunt think otherwise.

She went to the stable late that night, and as the horse raised his head at her coming she whispered. '*You* won't leave me, will you, Jasper? I said that you and Aunt Grace were the only things in my life that didn't change, but I was wrong, wasn't I? Now there's only you.'

Davina didn't tell Rowan about Grace's approaching wedding. He would know soon enough when he received his invitation, and in the meantime she didn't want him feeling sorry for her or asking questions.

When Grace had said that she was going to invite him, Davina had said, 'I'd rather you didn't.'

'Why, for heaven's sake?' her aunt had exclaimed. 'He will be company for you for one thing, and for another I'm going to ask him to give me away as there is no other man in my life I can ask. Hopefully, when we get him into the wedding atmosphere, he might have a change of mind about you.'

Davina sighed. 'I don't want anyone to marry me just because he's got that wedding feeling. And in any case he might feel that his presence there would be an embarrassment and refuse the invitation.'

On a crisp autumn morning a week later Rowan came into Davina's room with the invitation in his hand and a surprised look on his face.

'You never told me that Grace was going to be married!' he exclaimed. 'I take it that this is the guy she was seeing the night we…'

'Nearly overstepped the mark?' she prompted dryly. 'What a lucky escape that was, wasn't it?'

'Very funny. I'm glad you see something humorous in

what happened. But getting back to this.' He waved the invitation under her nose. 'What about it?'

'What do you mean?'

'I mean why didn't you tell me that Grace is getting married? You're going to be all alone in that big house.'

'So?'

'So, I don't like the idea.'

'That's the reason why I didn't tell you. I don't want you fussing.'

'Fussing!' he hissed angrily. 'Concern comes under a different label than ''fussing''. It's lonely up there on the hillside. There are one or two frisky types I can think of in the area who might just decide to pay you a visit when they know you're all alone.'

She shrugged and his irritation increased.

'Do you have to be so aggravating?'

'What do you want me to say? That I'm terrified of the prospect? The thing that will affect me the most is not having Aunt Grace around, but I'll get used to it. I'll end up being one of those old maids who cling to the family home and the bits of silver because they've got nothing else to love.'

She was being deliberately irritating and knew it, but she couldn't stop herself. There was an urge in her to hit out for the misery he was putting her through.

When he came round the desk and, taking her arm, yanked her to her feet, instead of making the most of the sudden contact, she said, 'I could always take in lodgers.'

'Who, for instance?' he said through tight lips.

'Well, if all these ''frisky types'' are going to be hanging around, maybe they would do for starters.'

'Don't play with me, Davina,' he said coldly, as if the fire of his anger had turned to ice. 'If you think I'm enjoying keeping away from you, you're very much mistaken. The number of times in a day I have to resist the urge to take you somewhere away from here and forget about who I am are countless. But for the moment let's put *this* on to my account.'

Within seconds of his mouth bonding with hers Davina's arms were around his neck, her breasts springing to life against his chest, but they both knew it couldn't last. They were in the surgery of all places. Any moment someone would appear.

As they drew apart she gasped, '*Are* you going to accept Grace's invitation?'

'Do by all means bring us back to earth,' he groaned. 'In answer to the question, I'm not sure. I'm supposed to be keeping a low profile where your family are concerned.'

'Really! So what just happened was *you* keeping a low profile?'

'That…and indulging myself.'

There were footsteps outside in the passage and she said quickly, 'You'll have to come to the wedding. Grace is going to ask you to give her away.'

'That will be one of the nicest things that has ever happened to me,' he said gravely. 'It shows that *she* bears me no ill will.'

'Neither of us do, Rowan,' she said softly as tears pricked. 'Why can't you see that?'

'Yes, but it's not me that Grace will be marrying,' he said in the same sombre tone, and Davina had no answer to that.

That evening, after he'd eaten, Rowan's thoughts turned to the wedding. The invitation said it was to take place in October, which was only weeks away, so the happy couple were wasting no time.

He'd been dumbstruck to hear that Grace was getting married and leaving the country, and he wasn't all that happy about it. He'd felt that no matter what he said or did Davina would always have Grace to turn to, but that was about to change.

When he'd expressed his worries about her living alone she'd mocked him, and he supposed he couldn't blame her. She must be thinking that his concern was somewhat overdue. That he didn't care how miserable he was making her, but wasn't pleased to hear that she was going to be living alone in the future.

There was a grim smile on his face as he recalled her taunt about taking in lodgers. At least he hoped that was what it had been. That she wasn't serious!

The irony of the situation was that he had only to put his scruples to one side and the problem of her living alone would be solved.

Grace had called at the practice during the afternoon to ask him to give her away and he'd found that she wasn't happy about leaving Davina on her own either. She hadn't suggested that he get his act together in so many words, but she'd given him food for thought by saying, 'If Davina decides there is nothing to keep her here, I shall try to persuade her to practise medicine in the States.'

It had been said casually, but he'd got the message and he'd thought bleakly that she must be thinking that her elderly American could set him an example in not beating about the bush.

But the Texan was a lucky man. He came with a clean slate.

*   *   *

In the weeks leading up to Grace's wedding Davina didn't have time to mope at the thought of her going to live in Texas. There was so much to do.

The ceremony was to take place in the big stone church that dominated the valley. Caterers had been hired for the reception at Heatherlea and in the middle of what seemed like an endless list of arrangements the two women had bought their outfits.

A smart dress and jacket in the palest of blues had been Grace's choice and Davina's was a full-skirted, calf-length dress of oyster silk.

When Rowan asked what she would be wearing, she said perversely, 'Why do you want to know? I'm under the impression that weddings aren't much in your line.' And watched his expression close up at the pert reply.

The feeling of rejection was never far away and she thought that it was just too bad if he didn't realise it. Within the practice they were a team, working together for the good of those who needed them, but outside it Davina felt as if they were living at opposite ends of the world so little did they meet socially.

On an overcast Sunday afternoon in early October Davina was saddling Jasper up when Grace appeared.

'Where are you off to?' she asked anxiously, eyeing the darkening sky above.

'Just a quick gallop up to the cross,' Davina replied. 'I feel as if I need some fresh air.'

If she'd been truthful she would have said that she wanted to be alone, that she needed time to think. But Grace was watching her like a hawk these days on the lookout for any signs that she wasn't as happy as she was making out. And a heart to heart was the last thing that Davina felt she wanted to face.

The old stone cross at the top of the hill had always

been the place where she went to in times of trouble. Legend had it that there'd once been a monastery there and the cross was all that was left of it.

She was used to the weather changes in the valley, knew the signs as well as she knew her own face, and was confident she would be back before the elements ran amok.

'Don't worry, I won't be long,' she promised, and, hoisting herself up onto Jasper's back, she cantered off.

There'd been a communication in Saturday morning's post regarding a vacancy at a practice in the city. The partners there would be interviewing during the following week and she didn't know whether to go.

A move at this time wasn't ideal, with Grace's wedding coming up. That was a big enough change in her life and to move to another practice at the same time would feel as if everything that mattered was being taken away from her.

But, she thought glumly as she reined to a halt beside the old stone cross, the thing that mattered most had already been taken from her. Without Rowan in her life she was lost. Some people would say that working with him was better than nothing and she supposed it was, but they could have something much better if he would only unbend.

The sky above was dark and miserable in keeping with her mood, she thought. As the first drops of rain began to fall she started to guide Jasper back down the hill.

By the time they were halfway it was as black as night and the rain was falling thick and fast. When something leapt out of a tree to land in front of them she could only see its shape in the gloom for a stricken moment, and then Jasper was rearing up on his hind legs in fright and she was being catapulted off his back.

*   *   *

Rowan had also been out in the open, walking the tops deep in his own thoughts. When it began to cloud over he decided that it would be a good time to call on Grace to discuss his duties at the wedding and any other matters she might require assistance with.

His main reason for calling was to see Davina. Even though they'd been in each other's company at the practice for most of the week, he still found it difficult getting through the weekends without a sighting of her.

When Grace opened the door to him she was looking anxious and he asked, 'What's wrong? You look worried.'

'I am,' she said, stepping back to let him. 'Davina's out on Jasper and any moment the heavens are about to open.'

'Where has she gone?'

'To the cross on the top of the hill. She knew a storm was coming and said she wouldn't be long.'

'I shouldn't worry,' he said reassuringly. 'She'll be back any moment. You'll see.'

He didn't like the idea of Davina being out on Jasper beneath those lowering skies either, but no one knew the valley better than she did.

Grace made tea and they chatted about the wedding and all the time he was looking out of the window and keeping his eye on the clock.

By now the storm was in full force and he couldn't sit there any longer.

'I'm going to look for her, Grace,' he said. 'And if she comes back in the meantime, make sure she stays put and doesn't come looking for me.'

As he went up the hill the deluge continued, but it was getting lighter as the stormclouds passed. He had an awful feeling that something had happened to Davina, and every time he thought of the possibilities his stomach knotted.

He could see the cross in the distance and he quickened his step. If she wasn't up there he wasn't sure where to look next. The first thing he saw as he turned a bend in the path was Jasper standing guard beside the still figure of his mistress. Rowan broke into a run.

They were both soaked to the skin and Davina was moaning softly, her eyes closed. When he flung himself down beside her and said her name, she opened them and gazed up at him blearily.

'Where am I?' she croaked.

'It looks as if Jasper has thrown you,' he said gently. 'Don't move until I've checked that you haven't broken anything.'

She was struggling to sit up.

'I'm all right, Rowan. The fall knocked me out, but I can move everything, I think.'

'Has he ever done this kind of thing before?' he asked tightly.

'No. Never. He wouldn't have done it today if something hadn't leapt out at us from the trees and frightened him.'

He helped her carefully to her feet. There was a gash on her temple and the blood from it was running down her cheek in watery rivulets. Her face was deathly pale and she was shivering with the cold.

'I've got to get you home as fast as I can,' he said grimly, 'or you'll have pneumonia to add to your aches and pains. There's no way anyone could get a car or the ambulance up here, so do you think Jasper will let you mount him again?'

'Yes, of course he will,' she mumbled through chattering teeth. 'It wasn't his fault that the phantom animal jumped out in front of him.'

'We'll discuss that aspect of events when we get you home and dry,' he said briskly. 'Now, let's see if we can get you onto his back again.'

Davina felt terrible, but wasn't going to admit it. Every bone in her body ached. But at least none of them appeared to be broken, and her hard hat had saved her head.

As Rowan led Jasper carefully back the way they had come, she gave her full attention to the horse, patting him gently and telling him how special he was and how she would never forget the way he'd stayed with her.

Davina had more rapport with Jasper than she had with *him*, he thought grimly as he listened. Maybe she felt that Jasper's unconditional affection was more acceptable than his own tortured reasoning.

The moment Grace saw the bedraggled trio stop in front of the house the door was flung open and she was out there, exclaiming anxiously, 'What's happened?'

Rowan was lifting Davina down with gentle hands and now, too chilled to the bone to be able to speak, she was ready to let him do the talking.

'The mysterious animal leapt out at them. Jasper reared up in fright and threw Davina,' he told Grace, still tense with the horror of finding her lying there beside the horse.

When they'd helped her inside, Grace hurried upstairs to run a hot bath and he said, 'Once you've warmed up and put on some dry clothes, I'm going to give you a good checking over, Davina.'

Her gaze was on Jasper, standing meekly outside the front porch in the driving rain.

'See to Jasper first, please, Rowan,' she begged tearfully. 'He's wet through. If anything happens to him

I'll have lost everything. That "thing" out there was after him.'

'When you've got cleaned up and have thawed out we'll talk about it,' he said gently. As Grace called down that a hot bath was ready he added, 'Go and soak all the cold out of you and I'll do as you ask.' He gave a wry smile. 'I never thought I'd be up against a horse for your affections.'

She managed a smile of her own.

'You don't have to compete with anybody. But I've offered myself on a plate once too often. The ball is in your court, Dr Westlake.'

There was much bruising but no obvious damage when Rowan examined Davina. The cut on the temple was more of a graze than a gash and would heal without stitching.

When Davina was finally settled by the fire, wrapped in a warm robe and with a mug of hot tea in her hands, he said, 'So tell us about this animal, Davina. What did it look like? How big was it? What colour? And was it really up in the tree?'

'Yes,' she told him, shuddering at the memory. 'The rain had just started to come down really heavily and it had gone very dark when suddenly it came hurtling down on us with teeth bared and eyes gleaming. When Jasper reared up and I screamed, it must have been frightened off. I was conscious of it scampering away through the trees as I was falling. After that I don't recall anything until I looked up and saw you bending over me. You were a most welcome sight.'

'Something has got to be done about this!' Grace exclaimed indignantly.

Rowan nodded sombrely. 'Indeed it has. The whole thing has gone beyond a joke. Describe it to us, Davina.'

'It was so dark out there on the hillside I didn't get a very good look at it, but it *was* like a cat.'

'A domestic tabby?'

'It had the colouring of some cats I've seen, tawny with indistinct black spotting. But it was a lot bigger than the cats we know and much fiercer to look at.'

'I'm going to phone the police, the peak wardens, mountain rescue team and anyone else I can think of,' Rowan said grimly. 'It was obviously out to attack Jasper and you but was scared off by the rumpus you both created. Supposing it had been children out there, they wouldn't have stood a chance. For its own sake as well as everyone else's, this cat thing has to be caught.'

The thought of Davina's youthful beauty being savaged by the jaws of some predator was making him feel physically sick and at the same time weak with protective tenderness.

Until this thing was caught he would never have a moment's peace of mind, especially after Grace had gone and Davina was alone in this rambling place.

So do something about it, common sense said, but he could imagine the interpretation Davina would put on a change of heart at this particular moment. She wasn't going to melt at a proposal that was motivated by concern more than anything else.

As if reading his thoughts, she got to her feet. Tightening the wrap around her, she said, 'I'm going upstairs to get dressed, and as soon as the storm passes I'm going out on Jasper again.'

'I don't think so,' he said levelly. 'As your doctor I don't advise it. You've had quite a shaking up and should spend the rest of the day taking things quietly.'

'*I* am my doctor,' she retorted, 'and I have to get up on Jasper again as soon as I can. I've never been thrown before and I don't want to lose my nerve.'

'You've already been back up on him,' he said exasperatedly, with the feeling that he was being tested in some way.

'Yes, but not to ride in the full sense.'

'So you're not bothered that I'm concerned about you.'

She shrugged and he could have shaken her.

'I'm only going to be riding up and down the lane outside.'

'Suit yourself,' he snapped, and, picking up his jacket, he flashed a smile in Grace's direction and departed.

'That wasn't very nice,' Grace said when he'd gone. 'That man was showing concern on your behalf and you behaved most offhandedly towards him. Rowan was quite right. You *should* take it easy for the rest of the day. *And* I don't remember hearing you thank him for bringing you home safely. You were more concerned about Jasper than the fact that Rowan had got a soaking on your behalf *and* been worried sick into the bargain.'

'I know,' Davina agreed penitently. 'But Jasper was in danger because I'd taken him up there. He had no choice. Rowan didn't *have* to come looking for me. I'd rather he did things for me of his own free will, not because he feels duty-bound.'

What she really meant was that she didn't want to feel under an obligation to him and her insistence that she was going out on Jasper again before the light faded had been one way of showing him that if he wanted to start issuing orders it had better be because he had the right to do so.

Yet underneath she was ashamed of her behaviour and

in the end she didn't go out on Jasper again. Rowan had been right. She *had* mounted the horse again, up there on the hillside, *and* ridden him home after a fashion. There would be no problem the next time she came to mount him.

But instead of resting, as Rowan had advised her to do, she found that she couldn't relax because of the churlish way she'd treated him, and after prowling the house restlessly for most of the evening she eventually picked up the phone.

When he heard her voice he said immediately, 'What's wrong, Davina? Not some injury from the fall that we didn't pick up on, is it?'

'No,' she replied, feeling even more ashamed at his obvious concern. 'I'm ringing to apologise. I behaved like a moron this afternoon. For one thing I never thanked you for coming to find me. You once said that you didn't deserve me. Well, today the boot was on the other foot. Am I forgiven?'

'Yes, of course you're forgiven. I could forgive you anything. You'd had an unpleasant experience and were understandably overwrought.'

'So you didn't think my petulance was anything to do with what *isn't* going on between us?'

After a moment's silence he said, 'Was it?'

'Oh, for goodness' sake, Rowan! Are you blind?'

'No. I'm not blind,' he said slowly. 'I see all too clearly. That's the problem.'

'So why were you at the house this afternoon in the first place?'

'I called to discuss my wedding duties with Grace.'

'I see. So the fact that you ended up having to save me was an extra facct of your visit.'

'If you want to see it like that...yes.'

He supposed if he had any brains he would tell her he'd felt he couldn't last until Monday without seeing her, and that he'd been disappointed to find her not there.

For the rest of it he'd just been grateful that his longing had taken him there and that he'd been able to bring her back to safety.

'I'll see you tomorrow,' she was saying. 'At least at the practice we're on the same wavelength.' And before he could reply she had hung up.

Rowan had made the phone calls he'd thought necessary when he'd got back home in the gathering dusk and thought afterwards that a wet Sunday afternoon in October was hardly the best time for rallying the troops.

Jim, the village bobby, had said he would be on the lookout and would pass the message on to his superiors. There was no reply from the mountain rescue headquarters, so obviously they were all out somewhere in the rugged countryside. One of the peak wardens was on holiday and the other had just got in wet through and was in no mood for venturing forth again.

All of which had made him decide that he would ring again in the morning as it was quite clear that it hadn't been a blundering young bullock this time. But what *had* it been?

Certainly not a puma from the sound of it but a wild creature nonetheless, and hunger would make it venture forth where a well-fed animal might not be so inclined.

In the brief conversation he'd had with Grace before going to search for Davina, he'd discovered that there were to be no top hats and morning suits at the wedding. Just smart suits for the bridegroom, his best man, who was one of Wesley's business associates in the United Kingdom, and himself.

Quite a few of the valley people had been invited and he'd thought whimsically that it would be like a day at the surgery only they would be in their Sunday best.

After Davina's phone call he'd had more food for thought and none of it was very palatable. He didn't blame her for being disenchanted with him. She'd made that clear twice in one day. But if she was miserable, so was he. The only difference was that his misery was self-inflicted.

CHAPTER ELEVEN

DURING a restless night Rowan came to two decisions. One was that he wasn't going to rest until the animal on the loose had been found. The other was regarding an idea that had been in his mind for some time and that he was now going to put into practice, subject to the approval of someone else.

While Davina was busy with her patients next morning, he called Alan Marsh, a volunteer with the mountain rescue team. He had a wide knowledge of the terrain of the area and if he could throw no light on the mysterious prowler, at least he could put him in the picture with the previous day's happening and ask Alan and his colleagues to be on the lookout.

To his surprise the man needed no convincing that there was a dangerous animal on the loose. It appeared that the team had been out on exercises all day Sunday, and on their way back they'd come across the remains of a young deer.

'We found it on the edge of the Latimer estate,' Rowan was told. 'There were some strange pawprints in the mud that the rain had caused, and none of us had ever seen anything like them before. They were twice the size of those of a domestic cat, with retractable claws and four oval toe prints. A bit like those of a coyote or a dog, but more rounded. We got on to the authorities immediately and left it at that.'

'We shall be on the lookout, needless to say, but when a wild creature is on the loose it can be just about anywhere, and if it is capable of killing a deer it's no weakling. It's strange how it came to leap from above out of the trees, and from the way it's been described to you it does seem to have catlike tendencies, but on a larger and more vicious scale.'

When he'd replaced the receiver Rowan was even more concerned about Davina's safety. If the thing could slaughter a deer, could it kill a horse? He doubted it, but there was nothing to say that it couldn't.

After surgery he said to Davina, 'I want you with me on my first call of the day.'

She observed him with wide and wary eyes. It was usually she who asked for his assistance.

'What's the problem?' she asked, with the previous day's ups and downs still fresh in her mind.

'There *is* no problem regarding that. I'll tell you when we get there. But I do have a problem about something else, like what occurred yesterday.'

'Why? What's happened now?'

'The mountain rescue guys found the carcass of a young deer late yesterday afternoon. It would appear that the creature went looking elsewhere after stalking Jasper and you.'

'Ugh! How dreadful!' she exclaimed. 'Whatever could it be that can bring a deer down?'

'Good question,' he said grimly. 'They found some strange prints at the scene. Rounded toes, no claws, twice as big as those of a domestic cat. So the mystery deepens. You will take care, won't you, Davina? If it got the smell of Jasper in its nostrils it might come back, and I can't bear the thought of anything happening to you.'

'And I can't bear the thought of anything happening to Jasper,' she told him as the colour drained from her face. 'Let's go,' she begged. 'I don't want to talk about it any more. I hope you haven't got any more unpleasant tidings to impart.'

Rowan was smiling now. 'That will depend on how you view my next announcement.'

'Now you've got me curious.'

'Well, curious is better than furious any day. If you're ready, we'll be off.'

As she drove behind him along the main street of the village Davina was wondering which of their patients required the presence of two doctors. But Rowan wasn't stopping. He was driving to the other end of the valley, to where a small lake stood beside a tumbledown barn with the peaks in the background.

'It's too cold for a picnic,' she said inanely as she got out of the car and looked around her in bewilderment.

He didn't answer. Just pointed to the FOR SALE notice on the building.

'What?' she asked, her confusion increasing.

'I made an offer on this place first thing this morning, and just before we left they came back to me to say it has been accepted.'

'You're going to live here?'

'Yes, though not in its present condition. I'm fortunate that I can stay in the apartment until such time as we're ready to move in.'

'We?' she squeaked.

'Yes, us, Davina. I don't care a damn about my name any more. I never did. It was for your sake that I was so conscious of it. But I can't exist any longer without you.' His mouth curved into a smile. 'I want to make you an offer. It will be the second I've made today.'

'And what's that?' she asked weakly.

'Well, I know you must wish I had a different name, so I'm quite prepared to change it to something else if you'll forgive me for the unhappiness I've caused you...and be my wife. That's if you can bear the thought of leaving Heatherlea.'

'Of course I can bear to leave Heatherlea,' she said with radiance all around her. 'If we're going to bury the past once and for all, a new start is exactly what we need. And how did you know I'd always thought this a divine place?'

'I didn't. I just hoped that for once I was doing something right. But you haven't answered my question.'

'I know. Before I do there is something *I* want to ask *you*.'

'Yes?'

'Are you doing this because of yesterday, or because Grace is leaving and you're labouring under a mistaken sense of responsibility?'

'Do you mean do I go weak with terror at the thought of anything happening to you? Yes, but that's not the only reason. You know very well I love you, Davina. Have done ever since that first morning when you looked down at me from Jasper's back and invited me to breakfast. Sadly, at that moment I had no idea of the rocky road ahead, but if you'll only say you'll marry me, we'll make our own smooth pathway.'

They were feet apart, not even touching, but now she began to walk slowly towards him. And as the bright gaze that was the first thing she'd noticed about him was fixed on her, she held out her arms.

As he moved into the circle of them she said, 'Yes, I'll marry you, Rowan. I thought you'd never ask. And I don't want you to change your name. After all, what is it? Just an arrangement of letters.'

It was Grace's wedding day and Heatherlea was filled with happiness and flowers. Ever since she'd known that there would soon be another wedding, the bride to be had been radiant.

'I can leave you with an easy mind now,' she'd said when they'd told her their news.

'And you won't mind having to come back again soon for *our* wedding?' Davina had asked.

'Just try and stop me,' Grace had said joyfully. And now her own special day had arrived.

An autumn sun was beaming down as guests and well-wishers arrived at the church, and in the house not far away Grace, Davina and Rowan were preparing to leave for the ceremony.

It was to be Davina's last day in her old home. To-night, after Grace and Wes had boarded their flight to Texas, she would move into Rowan's apartment until such time as the house by the lake was ready.

She had no regrets. The past had brought her the future and Rowan Westlake *was* her future.

The last few guests were drifting off and the caterers were clearing away. Rowan was driving Grace and Wesley to the airport while Davina stayed behind to make sure that everyone had transport home and the trappings of the wedding were removed.

She and Grace had made their farewells with thankful hearts and easy minds. The future had opened up for them both in ways that neither of them had dreamed of.

Once the house was empty Davina walked slowly to the stable. She would have to come back each day to see to Jasper until he moved into his new quarters, but that would be all. Heatherlea would be sold soon.

Glad to have a few moments on her own, she saddled him and went for a quick gallop, keeping a watch on the time as she didn't want to be missing when Rowan returned.

Back at the stable she removed the saddle and began to lead him towards the door, ready to secure him for the night. But he was pulling back, whinnying loud and tossing his head.

She eyed him in perplexity. What was wrong? There was no vicious beast to scare him today. She tried again to lead him into the stable but to no avail. It was then that she saw eyes glowing in the shadowed interior and she froze.

It was in there! Must have gone in while they'd been away. Jasper could smell it. With her heart in her mouth she stepped forward and slammed the stable door shut, then locked it.

She was shaking. It was typical that something like this should spoil the beautiful day.

Jasper was quiet now and as she patted him gently she heard Rowan call her name.

As she flew to his side he said, 'The newly-weds are safely on their way, Davina. We can relax.'

'Not yet!' she croaked. 'It's in the stable, Rowan!'

'What is?'

'The cat thing. I've locked it in there.'

'What?' he gasped.

He took her hand and they raced back to where Jasper was tethered outside the stable.

They could hear it now, scratching and howling, and he asked in slow amazement, 'How did it get in there?'

'I'd taken Jasper for a quick gallop and when we came back he wouldn't go in. The thing must have crept in while we were away and he sensed its presence.'

'I'm going to get some help,' he said, 'and you're coming with me. I'm not letting you out of my sight while that wild thing is around.'

They'd been and gone—the police, the RSPCA and a local wildlife expert who had identified the imprisoned animal as a bobcat or wildcat, normally found in southern Canada.

They'd been viewing it through a small opening light in the roof and he'd said, 'These cats roam scrub or bushy hillsides such as these. They feed on squirrels, hares, birds and the occasional deer. As you all saw, it was a big fellow, a male, and I surmise that it was smuggled over here as someone's pet and then thrown out when it got too big. It's cruel, but folk do it all the time. They fancy an exotic pet and then ditch it when the novelty has worn off.'

'So the poor thing was just as much sinned against as sinning,' Davina had commented. 'What will happen to it now?'

One of the officials had sedated it with a tranquilliser gun through the roof opening and it had soon become limp and unresisting.

'I imagine that one of the zoos will take it,' he'd said. 'I'm sure you won't be sorry to see it go.'

'There are three of us who agree on that,' Rowan had told him, 'my fiancée, myself and Jasper.'

And now they were alone at last. They'd locked up at Heatherlea and Davina was settling into the apartment.

Rowan had suggested a few times that if she wanted they could live at Heatherlea until the barn conversion was done, instead of her having to put up with the small confines of his own accommodation. But she'd told him each time, 'Heatherlea is the past. *You* are my future. Where you are, I want to be. I don't care where it is, just as long as we're together.'

Modern Romance™
...seduction and
passion guaranteed

Tender Romance™
...love affairs that
last a lifetime

Medical Romance™
...medical drama
on the pulse

Historical Romance™
...rich, vivid and
passionate

Sensual Romance™
...sassy, sexy and
seductive

Blaze Romance™
...the temperature's
rising

27 new titles every month.

Live the emotion

MILLS & BOON®

MB3

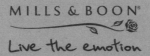

MILLS & BOON®

Live the emotion

Medical Romance™

OUTBACK ENCOUNTER *by Meredith Webber*

As a research scientist, Dr Caitlin O'Shea's usual problem is not being taken seriously – her stunning blonde looks get in the way! But she's not expecting her work in tiny Outback town Turalla to have so many other challenges – like Connor Clarke, the town's overworked doctor…

THE NURSE'S RESCUE *by Alison Roberts*

Paramedic Joe Barrington was determined not to give in to his attraction for nurse Jessica McPhail – he just couldn't get involved with a mother, and Jessica had to put her child Ricky first. But when Joe risked his life to rescue Ricky, he and Jessica realised that the bond between them was growing stronger by the day.

A VERY SINGLE MIDWIFE *by Fiona McArthur*

Beautiful midwife Bella Wilson has recently regained her independence – and she doesn't want obstetrician Scott Rainford confusing things. Twelve years ago their relationship ended painfully, and she won't let him hurt her all over again. But now, working side by side, they find their feelings for each other are as strong as ever...

On sale 6th February 2004

Available at most branches of WHSmith, Tesco, Martins, Borders, Eason, Sainsbury's and all good paperback bookshops.

0104/03a

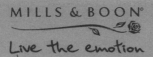

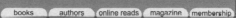

4 FREE

books and a surprise gift!

We would like to take this opportunity to thank you for reading this Mills & Boon® book by offering you the chance to take FOUR more specially selected titles from the Medical Romance™ series absolutely FREE! We're also making this offer to introduce you to the benefits of the Reader Service™—

★ FREE home delivery
★ FREE gifts and competitions
★ FREE monthly Newsletter
★ Exclusive Reader Service offers
★ Books available before they're in the shops

Accepting these FREE books and gift places you under no obligation to buy, you may cancel at any time, even after receiving your free shipment. Simply complete your details below and return the entire page to the address below. *You don't even need a stamp!*

YES! Please send me 4 free Medical Romance books and a surprise gift. I understand that unless you hear from me, I will receive 6 superb new titles every month for just £2.60 each, postage and packing free. I am under no obligation to purchase any books and may cancel my subscription at any time. The free books and gift will be mine to keep in any case.

M4ZED

Ms/Mrs/Miss/Mr ....Initials.....................................
BLOCK CAPITALS PLEASE

Surname ....

Address ....

....

....Postcode................................

Send this whole page to:
UK: FREEPOST CN81, Croydon, CR9 3WZ
EIRE: PO Box 4546, Kilcock, County Kildare (stamp required)

Offer valid in UK and Eire only and not available to current Reader Service subscribers to this series. We reserve the right to refuse an application and applicants must be aged 18 years or over. Only one application per household. Terms and prices subject to change without notice. Offer expires 30th April 2004. As a result of this application, you may receive offers from Harlequin Mills & Boon and other carefully selected companies. If you would prefer not to share in this opportunity please write to The Data Manager at the address above.

Mills & Boon® is a registered trademark owned by Harlequin Mills & Boon Limited.
Medical Romance™ is being used as a trademark.
The Reader Service™ is being used as a trademark.